Hardcourt Upset

D0096669

The Chip Hilton Sports Series

For more information on
Chip Hilton-related activities and to correspond
with other Chip Hilton fans, check the website at
www.chiphilton.com

Chip Hilton Sports Series
#15

Hardcourt Upset

Coach Clair Bee
Updated by Randall and Cynthia Bee Farley
Foreword by Jack McCallum

BROADMAN
& HOLMAN
PUBLISHERS

Nashville, Tennessee

0-8054-2094-0

Published by Broadman & Holman Publishers,
Nashville, Tennessee

Subject Heading: BASKETBALL—FICTION / YOUTH

Library of Congress Cataloging-in-Publication Data

Registration information has been provided to the Library of
Congress, Washington, D.C.

1 2 3 4 5 04 03 02 01 00

DR. TERRING HEIRONIMUS

surgeon, friend, and teammate
whose life has been an inspiration to all those who know him.

CLAIR BEE, 1957

ALAN REID, P.A.

As Dr. Heironimus helped Clair Bee with his original manuscripts,
we thank you for so generously assisting us.

RANDY AND CINDY
2000

Contents

CONTENTS

Foreword

IT'S SOMETIMES difficult to figure out why we became who we became. Was it an influential teacher who steered you toward biology? A beloved grandparent who turned you into a machinist? A motorcycle accident that forced you into accounting?

All I know is that in my case the Chip Hilton books had something—no, a lot—to do with my becoming a sports journalist. At the very least, the books got me to sit down and read when others of my generation were watching television or otherwise goofing off; at most, they taught me many of life's lessons, about sports and sportsmanship, about coaches and coaching, about winning and losing.

Also, the books helped me, quite literally, get the job I have now. Over two decades ago, when I was a sports writer at a small newspaper in Pennsylvania, I interviewed Clair Bee and wrote a piece about him and the Hilton books. For some strange reason, even before I met Clair, I knew I could make the story memorable, knew that meeting a legend like Clair and plumbing his mind for memories were going to be magic. They were. I sold the story to *Sports Illustrated,* and, partly because of it, I was later hired there full time.

To my surprise, and especially to the surprise of the editors at *SI,* the story produced a torrent of letters, hundreds of them, all written by closet Clair and Chip fans who, like me, had grown up on the books and never been able to forget them. Since the piece about Clair appeared in 1979, I've written hundreds of other articles, many of them cover stories about famous athletes like Michael Jordan, Magic Johnson, and Larry Bird; yet I'm still known, by and large, as the "guy who wrote the Chip Hilton story." I would safely say that still, two decades later, six months do not go by that I don't receive some kind of question about Clair and Chip.

One of the many fortunate things that happened to me as a result of that story was meeting Clair's daughter, Cindy Farley, and her husband, Randy, as well as others who could recite the starting lineups of Coach Rockwell's Valley Falls teams.

I am proud to have played a small part in the revival of Chip and the restoration of interest in Clair (not that real basketball people ever forget him). It's hard to put a finger on what exactly endures from the books, but it occurs to me that what Clair succeeded in doing was to create a universe of which we would all like to be a part.

As I leafed through one of the books recently, a memory came back to me from my days as a twelve-year-old Pop Warner football player in Mays Landing, New Jersey. A friend who shared my interest in the books had just thrown an opposing quarterback for a loss in a key game. As we walked back to the huddle, he put his arm on my shoulder pads and, conjuring up a Hilton gang character, whispered, "Another jarring tackle by Biggie Cohen." No matter how old you get, you never forget something like that. Thank you, Clair Bee.

JACK McCALLUM
Senior Writer, *Sports Illustrated*

CHAPTER 1

Doctor's Orders

CHIP HILTON perched on the edge of the examination table as Dr. Mike Terring, State University's team physician, examined his injured knee. Terring lifted the varsity star's leg, straightened it out, and then pressed the knee with his fingertips here and there, asking the same questions over and over: "Hurt? . . . No? . . . How about this?"

Chip wiped his damp forehead with the back of his hand and shook his head. "No, Doc, it just hurts a little when I bend my leg." Dr. Terring carried a sheaf of X rays across the room and held each print up to the light. He scrutinized each with minute care, one by one.

Chip rocked nervously back and forth, holding his right knee between the long fingers of his locked hands. It was cool in the room, but perspiration beaded across his forehead. Beside the table, Soapy Smith, Chip's lifelong friend, shifted restlessly from one foot to the other and solemnly watched, his eyes darting anxiously between the physician and the X rays.

Dr. Terring appeared to be satisfied at last and walked back to the table. He tossed the X rays on the counter and hooked his thumbs in the pockets of his lab coat. "Well, Chip, there's nothing broken or chipped. But the ligament is badly swollen."

"Then it isn't the cartilage?"

"Nope! Strained ligament. It can be pretty painful."

"I don't mind the pain."

Dr. Terring peered over his glasses and grinned. "No? Well, my boy, if you use this knee for basketball, you'll take that back. You've got to cut out the running."

"In other words, no basketball," Chip said grimly.

Mike Terring nodded. "That's right."

"But I've got to play, Doc. We've got a chance to win the conference. Maybe the NCAA title."

"He's gotta defend his marksmanship title too," Soapy added.

Dr. Terring grunted and studied the knee again, pressing gently on the joint. "I know, I know," he said testily, "but I don't like it. Shooting around a little might help, providing you got enough rest. But running and jumping and turning and cutting—no!"

Chip gripped the table fiercely. "But couldn't I be careful of it when I play, Doc? It doesn't hurt very much."

"Doesn't hurt? Is that so? Well, let's see." Terring grasped the knee again. "All right here? . . . Here? . . . And here? But how about this?" He pressed the side of the knee sharply and watched Chip's reaction.

Chip winced and unconsciously raised off the table just a little despite his efforts to conceal the pain. "Ummm . . ." he grunted.

"That's what I was getting at," the doctor said dryly, his eyes boring straight into Chip's.

DOCTOR'S ORDERS

"But that's different from running, Doc," Soapy protested, placing a hand on Chip's shoulder.

"Not much different, Soapy," Terring said shortly. He studied Chip for a second and then continued slowly, "You athletes are all alike. Always in a hurry. Afraid you'll miss a practice or a game. Lots of kids ruin fine sports careers just because they're impatient and won't give an injury enough rest.

"I've seen kids cripple their arms for life by throwing a baseball from the center-field fence clear to home plate without warming up, or showing off in football by tackling without wearing the right equipment or spearing someone. And," he added significantly, raising his eyebrows, "I know of certain cases where an athlete made the mistake of using an injured leg when the doctor told him to lay off.

"Another thing! Don't you let any of this team hero stuff run away with you. It's good to win championships, but nobody wants you to win at the expense of your health. Besides, you've got two big years left. Seems to me you've done pretty good for a sophomore: all-American quarterback in football and MVP in the basketball tournament."

"But, Doc, you don't understand! I can't run out on the team."

"You mean *walk* out," Dr. Terring contradicted grimly. He paused and then said gently, "I don't want to scare you, Chip, but a strained ligament can be disastrous."

Dr. Terring walked over to a closet. Opening the door, he pulled out a brace and shook it in the air. "It's a little old and beat up, Chipper, but it will do. Now you wear this until we can get you a new one from the med center."

Under the physician's watchful eyes, Chip strapped the brace on his knee. Then, while he was pulling on his jeans, Dr. Terring continued. "A knee is a tricky animal, Chip. This one needs something to reduce the swelling and some ice—and a vacation—a vacation from practice. Good news, it won't interfere with going to classes," he chuckled.

"How much of a vacation, Doc?"

"Oh, a week or ten days." Mike Terring shrugged.

"But I can't miss that much basketball."

"I'm afraid you'll have to, Hilton. Let's put it this way. Today is the third of January. With the big part of the conference basketball schedule coming up in February, isn't it important for you to be in good shape for the stretch drive? Isn't it better to miss three or four games now than to miss the entire season, or in the absolute worst case, the rest of your career?"

"That's for sure, Dr. Terring. It's just that I'd like to play."

"I know, Chip. But a week or so won't ruin the whole season."

Chip shook his head uncertainly. "I guess not," he said ruefully. "I probably wouldn't be much good anyway. Should I keep wearing the brace?"

"Absolutely. And no practice of any kind."

Dr. Terring turned back to his desk, and Chip and Soapy walked slowly out of the exam room in the training area of Assembly Hall and along the hall toward the court. In the gym, pounding feet and joyous shouts reminded the two friends that State's varsity basketball team was busy at work.

Coach Jim Corrigan read the expression on the two dejected faces as Chip slowly walked toward center court. Soapy quietly sat in the first seat along courtside, worried about Chip and the team and completely forgetting about not making the team himself.

"Not a good session with the doc?" Corrigan smiled kindly.

"No, Coach," Chip said. "No practice for at least a week. I think I could go, but he says it might become more serious if I didn't follow his directions. But I'll be here to help out every day."

"Well, Rock and I'll meet after practice with Doc and get all the details. Since he did say no practice, let's remove the temptations. I know Chip Hilton. If I have you at practice, first you'd help the managers, then you'd be on the floor showing a teammate something, then it would be a little more, and then a few drills. Before you knew it, you'd be doing exactly what Mike Terring wants you to avoid."

"A week!" Chip groaned.

"Maybe more," Soapy added glumly.

Chip reached for the door to the street, but Soapy brushed past him and shouldered it open. An icy gust of wind and snow greeted the redhead. He caught his breath. "Wow!" he cried, pushing Chip back. "You stay here. I'll see if I can find someone to drive us to work."

Before he could protest, Soapy was gone. Chip shivered and walked slowly away from the door, feeling the cold air bite right through his sweater and jacket. Before he reached the trophy cases lining the wall, a breathless Soapy was back, his cheeks brilliant red.

"C'mon, Chip, hurry! We got a lift with one of the professors from the history department. He'd been working out in the weight room, and I caught him just before he pulled out of the lot. He's going right by Grayson's."

Chip hurried after his friend, hunching his shoulders against the sharp wind. Once inside the car, he breathed a sigh of relief. "Pretty cold," he ventured.

"Minus seven with the wind chill," the professor replied. "Now you know how Napoleon felt on the way to Moscow."

"Well, I don't know about Napoleon, but we sure appreciate the ride," Soapy said earnestly. "There's not many people out on a day like this."

"My pleasure," the driver said, eyeing Chip in the mirror. "Say, you're Chip Hilton, aren't you?"

"Yes, I am."

"I've read about that knee of yours in the paper. How soon do you expect to be back in the lineup?"

That was enough for Soapy. He took over, detailing the part Chip had played in State's triumphant march to the championship in the Holiday Invitational Tournament. Chip breathed a sigh of relief when the professor pulled up in front of Grayson's and let them out.

Just outside the store, on State Street, Chip and Soapy paused and viewed the interior through the window. Fred "Fireball" Finley and Philip "Whitty" Whittemore were serving several customers at the old-fashioned soda fountain, while other students were gathered around the big-screen TV watching the Bob Costas special on ESPN. Just inside the door, Soapy's hopeless crush, petite Mitzi Savrill, was making change for a customer. Chip grinned happily and opened the door.

Mitzi saw him first. "And thirty makes—Chip! What did the doctor say about your knee?"

"Nothing much, Mitzi."

Fireball and Whitty almost bumped heads as they turned. "What d'ya know?" Fireball cried. "We've got important company."

"The tall guy with the blond hair looks familiar," Whitty added. "Hey, wait! I know *him!* That's Chip Hilton!"

"That redhead talking to the cashier sure comes in here a lot," Fireball added. "I think he's got it bad for her."

"Well, you got that right!" Soapy retorted in a whisper.

"They probably dropped in for a visit," Fireball suggested. He watched Chip walk toward the stockroom. "How's the leg, Chipper?" he asked. "All right?"

"Pretty good, Fireball. Where's Isaiah?"

Finley nodded toward the rear of the store. "Stockroom."

"Meet you at Pete's after work," Whitty called. "OK?"

Chip nodded and went on to the stockroom. Inside, he found Isaiah Redding and Mr. Grayson, his boss. Grayson's had opened thirty years earlier as a small pharmacy. The pharmacy had expanded to include a retail operation providing everything from greeting cards to beach towels; it was a thriving operation. But the college kids were more interested in what he'd done with the adjoining area. Grayson's was now one of the most popular college spots in University. The food court and fountain served great food and ice cream, and the large-screen TV, relaxed atmosphere, and new sound system were a big draw.

"What's the verdict, Chip?" Mr. Grayson asked.

"Dr. Terring said I can't play for a week or so."

"What about working, walking around?"

"Walking is all right. But I can't—"

"I can use you as a relief cashier, Chip. You say the word."

"Oh, no, Mr. Grayson. My knee is all right. It's just the running and turning and stops and starts in basketball."

"All right, but take it easy."

Chip and his assistant, Isaiah, devoted the rest of the evening to clearing up the back orders that had piled up during the Christmas holidays. Isaiah headed out around nine o'clock, and then Chip entered the inventory on the computer. He was tired, and his knee was tight when Soapy, Fireball, and Whitty barged in.

"Come on!" Fireball urged. "Cindy's probably already at Pete's Place."

"And I'm starving," Soapy grinned, grabbing Chip's jacket off the back of the chair and holding it out to him. "Let's go!"

Pete's Place was only a short distance from Grayson's, but it seemed a mile to Chip's knee in the cold weather. The little restaurant was crowded when the four Grayson's friends filed in and joined Cindy Collins, Fireball's girlfriend, in a booth opposite the counter.

Teammate Jimmy Chung and Pete Thorpe, the owner of the restaurant, called out to Chip and hurried over to the table. "Hi ya, Chip," Jimmy said, gripping his friend's hand eagerly. "How's your leg?"

"All right, I guess. When did you get back?"

"This morning. Grandfather and Pop and Tommy send their regards." Jimmy nodded at Soapy, "Grandfather's still talking about you, Soapy! You made quite an impression on him."

"You gonna play Wednesday night?" Pete asked.

Chip shook his head. "Dr. Terring said not this week, and Coach doesn't want me at practice either."

"Well, sounds like Coach Corrigan knows what he's doing. Anyway, we're all glad you're walking around under your own power. Wow! We're gettin' busy. Take care of these guys, Jimmy. I'll get the counter."

The five friends took a long time eating their burgers and slurping their shakes. The restaurant was warm and cozy and the conversation interesting.

"It's later than I thought," Cindy finally murmured,

looking down at her watch. "Come on, Fireball, you and Whitty can walk me back to my dorm."

"I like it here," Whitty said drowsily. "Too bad we can't stay all night."

"Well, we can't," Chip said decisively. "Come on, Soapy, let's head back to the dorm."

"No way!" Soapy protested. "You're not walking in this with that knee. I'll call for a cab."

A few minutes later, a taxi appeared to take them to their dorm, Jefferson Hall. Chip and Soapy were both tired and only interested in getting to sleep. A quick E-mail home, and they both called it a day.

The next morning Soapy was, as usual, the first one up. Chip was breathing heavily, deep in sleep, as Soapy dressed quietly. He tiptoed out of the room and hurried down the flight of steps to the first floor. Jeff's residents were just beginning to come to life when Soapy opened the front door and dragged in the bundle of newspapers for the hall. Slipping one out of the bundle, Soapy ran upstairs and shook Chip until his eyes blinked open. "OK, Chipper, hit the deck."

While Chip was dressing, Soapy rustled through the sports pages of the *News* to see what was in the paper about the upcoming game with Tech. "Hey, Chip!" he said, tapping the paper excitedly. "Listen to this guy Locke. He's at it again. Listen! 'State should restrict its competition to schools in its own division.' How about that? This Locke never gets tired, does he?"

"He's got to write something, Soapy. You can't fill up a sports section with scores and stats."

"Sure, Chip, but it shouldn't be filled up with a lot of half-truths and innu—innu—" Soapy spread his hands and shrugged. "Well, with stuff like that. You better hurry. Hey! You're limping bad! Your leg all right?"

Chip nodded. "Sure, Soapy. It's always stiff in the morning, especially in this weather. It'll loosen up as soon as I do a little walking. I'm ready. Let's go."

Tuesday was one of Chip's busiest days for classes. Each class seemed to carry him to the most distant building on the campus. He had never noticed the long treks before. In fact, he had welcomed the outdoor breaks and fresh air. But not today. His knee stiffened up during the lectures, and the brace added to his discomfort. And his knee wasn't the only annoyance.

The students were in an upbeat mood and talking about their vacations: the dates they'd had, the concerts and dances they'd been to, the movies they'd seen, and the places they'd traveled. But they weren't overlooking Chip's part in the holiday basketball tournament in Springfield. They surrounded him at every opportunity.

"Nice going, Chip! You guys fooled every expert in the country."

"Don't know how you guys did it."

"It was simple. They didn't lose any games."

"Duh-huh!"

"You shouldn't be walking around so much. The architects that designed this campus must've been marathoners!"

"See you at the rally tonight. Better get your speech ready."

Chip tried to be pleasant with everyone, but it wasn't easy. And that afternoon, his science lab seemed to last forever. He was on his feet during most of the two and a half hours, and when it ended, he had a strong inclination to head for his room in Jeff. But he shrugged off the thought and started the hike across campus to Assembly Hall, stopping from time to time to rest. At last he reached the building and reported to Murph Kelly, State's head trainer.

Kelly iced Chip's knee for the next half-hour and then led the way to the gym and up into the bleachers to watch the varsity practice. As they watched, the veteran trainer kept up a running commentary about the players.

"Chip, this team is the ninth wonder of the world. But take 'em individually. With a couple of exceptions, they're just a bunch of ordinary ballplayers. Now take the seniors, Barkley, Thornhill, and Gowdy. They're average ballplayers." He patted Chip's arm. "Don't get me wrong, Chip, they're nice enough kids. But championship ballplayers? Uh-uh."

"But they won the tournament, Murph."

"Sure they did. But they had a bunch of upsets going for them, plus a lot of spirit and drive and some breaks. Chip, you know as well as I do that Southwestern is the best team in the country. We caught 'em by surprise with the zone press."

"But how about Dane and Southeastern and Templeton?"

Kelly continued as if he hadn't even heard Chip. "The juniors on the squad—King, Di Santis, Tucker, and Chung—well, they can be classed as fair reserves. Period!"

Chip shook his head vigorously. "You're wrong about Jimmy. He's great! He's the best ball handler I ever saw."

Kelly nodded in agreement. "You're absolutely right. The best *anyone* ever saw. Then we come to your group. The sophomores. The number-one player in that group is Chip Hilton. And they don't come any better."

Chip gave Kelly a friendly shove. "Hey! Stop!"

"The rest of the sophomores," Kelly continued imperviously, "Morris, Reardon, and Bollinger, have possibilities.

Especially Bollinger. The big guy was a conceited jerk last year. Had to be a ballplayer though. Six-nine in his stocking feet, and fast! And with a father who drummed basketball into him for nineteen years. Yep, had to be. The big guy has come a long way in spite of his old man."

Kelly grinned and nudged Chip. "Guess you think I'm disloyal to the team. Not so! Just been looking at basketball too long to classify this team as anything but lucky!"

CHAPTER 2

Soapied Again!

CHIP DIDN'T feel much like working that night, but he wasn't ready to accept his boss's offer of a chair job. When Chip accepted the responsibilities of a tough job, he believed in standing on his own two feet, good or bad. And the stockroom job was tough! That night Chip and his assistant kept going until nine o'clock. Then Isaiah left for home, and Chip wearily dropped down in the chair beside the desk. He scarcely looked up when Soapy burst through the door.

"You should've seen it, Chip. It was great! There must have been a thousand boxes on the bonfire. Lit up the whole campus. About everyone in school was there, I guess.

"Had the team up on a stage, and President Babcock made a speech and said the school was proud of the team, and he congratulated everyone, and then the cheerleaders and the marching band took over."

"The band? Even the band was there?"

"Sure! They played the school fight song, and the cheerleaders did their gymnastic routines and then led some cheers, and then Coach Corrigan and all the players made speeches. You should've heard—"

"Wait! Are you telling me Speed, Sky, and Jimmy made speeches?"

"Well, Speed and Bollinger didn't say much, but Jimmy was great. Corrigan introduced all the guys, but when Jimmy stood up, the crowd went nuts and cheered him for about five minutes. He didn't need an introduction."

"What did he say?"

"Nothing much. Just said you won the tournament."

"*I* won the tournament! Oh, no!"

"Oh, *yes!* He said State couldn't have made it to the finals if it hadn't been for your playing and that he wouldn't even have been in the championship game if you hadn't talked his father into letting him come back to school."

"He shouldn't have said that."

"Why not? It's true! Anyway, the crowd began hollering for you, and Coach Corrigan said you had been excused because of your knee, but that you would be all right in a few days. I hope, I hope."

"Me too," Chip said grimly.

"Oh! I forgot. Just before everything was over, a bunch of guys from Tech drove up in a couple of pickups and an SUV with a really loud sound system blaring their Tech songs. They made some speeches and were bragging about seven straight and they had a little rap song about State bein' number eight. It wasn't bad.

"Then some of *our* guys began wondering what that SUV would look like upside down, and you should've seen those Tech guys beat it out of there. Great fun! Well, back to work. Oh, by the way, Mitzi said I could use her car."

SOAPIED AGAIN!

"What for?"

"To drive you home after work."

"Drive me home?"

Soapy grinned delightedly. "Sure! It works out great. I drive you home and come back for Mitzi. Every night! We get through at 10:30, and she's never finished before 11:00 or 11:15. We'll even have time for a fast sandwich."

"How do you get home?"

"She drops me off on her way home."

Chip shook his head. "No way, Soapy. I'll walk."

"C'mon, Chip, you know I hardly ever get to see Mitzi except when she's working. You'd be helping out a pal and fueling his love life."

Chip grinned, "What love life? You mean love *wish*, don't you? Besides, I thought you were worried about *my* knee."

Soapy's face reddened until his freckles seemed to be dancing. "I am, Chip, I am. But this is one of those business terms I learned. You know, a win-win situation."

"I see," Chip said, pausing to enjoy his pal's embarrassment.

"Man, Chip, you know how I feel about Mitzi."

Chip nodded. "Sure. Sure, I know."

"Then it's OK?"

"I guess it has to be."

Soapy grinned happily and bolted for the door. "Great! Then we'll start tonight. See you later. Now I've got to ask Mitzi about using her car," he said mischievously.

Chip just laughed and knew he'd been "Soapied" again.

Pete's Place was unusually quiet when the Grayson's crowd arrived to grab something to eat after work. Pete took their orders, and Jimmy Chung slid in beside Fireball and Cindy in the booth.

"Heard you made a speech, Jimmy," Chip said. "What's the big idea?"

"Speech? Idea?" Jimmy echoed. "Oh, sure, everybody made speeches. You know something," he said, changing the subject, "I'm worried about the game tomorrow—"

"You'll kill 'em," Soapy said with a tight grimace.

"Right!" Fireball agreed. "So what that Tech has won seven games straight. What teams did they beat?"

"They beat Southern," Whittemore said. "That's more than we could do."

"Sure," Fireball agreed, "but that was the first game of the season, and Chip wasn't playing."

"Chip won't be playing tomorrow night either," Soapy added dourly.

"Tech *must* have something," Chip said in reflection. "It isn't very smart to underestimate *any* team."

"Well, playing on the home court is worth ten points," Soapy added. "That ought to help. Whoa, we've gotta go, Chip. Getting late. The car is outside."

"Car?" Fireball echoed. "What car? Where you guys going?"

"Mitzi's car," Soapy whispered mysteriously. "I'll tell you all about it sometime. All I can say now is that she's sending me on an important mission every night."

"I'll bet," Fireball said. "Does she even know about this *mission?*"

"It's true," Soapy said. "You guys want to go home too?"

"Not us," Whitty said, glancing at the clock. "We went through that eleven o'clock business all through football. Remember?"

Game tension began building up in Chip early the next morning. It was difficult to concentrate in his classes and later that afternoon at work. He and Soapy had a quick meal at Pete's Place at six o'clock and started out for the game. It was only seven o'clock when they reached Assembly Hall, but the crowd was already moving toward the entrance. Cars, festooned with red and blue State University pennants and decals, were parked in long rows along every street, and the parking lots surrounding Assembly Hall were filling up rapidly. Here and there in the crowd, Tech rooters carried pennants and talked loudly about their undefeated team.

"We should have been invited to the tournament."

"Yeah, seven in a row, and we weren't good enough. Guess our school is too small to play in this division."

"Our team's big. What's the size of the student body got to do with it?"

"Everything! Besides, a team has got to have *names*. We don't have any big names on our team."

"That's right! But we've got a *team*. And we're undefeated."

"Sure! Uninvited too!"

Soapy glanced resignedly at Chip as they reached the locker room. Chip stopped with his hand on the doorknob, listening to the banging of lockers and Murph Kelly's growling orders. Suddenly he turned. "Come on! I'll sit with you."

"But you're supposed to be on the bench."

"No, I'm not. I'd be in the way, Soapy. We'll sit up behind the north basket. Best seat in the house. I'll just tell Murph, and then we'll head up."

"Right!"

They followed the fans slowly up the steps and gained seats above the floor. Down below, the shining court looked like a glossy caramel. Chip glanced at the scoreboard. State's freshmen were giving the Tech team a trouncing. With a little over a minute left to play, the junior Statesmen were leading, 71-34. The comments he'd overheard from the Tech fans came to mind. Chip guessed they were right; there sure didn't seem to be any big-name stars playing on Tech's freshman team.

The preliminary game ended then, and the Tech varsity came trotting out. A burst of applause greeted them, but it was overwhelmed by the resounding roar that exploded as State's white-clad varsity dashed on the court. Chip's heart jumped, and he found himself on his feet beside Soapy and cheering for his teammates. He was so engrossed in watching Jimmy, Speed, Sky, Bitsy, Rudy Slater, and the veterans dashing through the warm-up drills that he didn't realize he was still standing after the fans around them had taken their seats.

Soapy tugged at Chip's sweater. "Chip! Sit down."

Chip glanced around sheepishly and sat down, still applauding. Then he concentrated on the Tech squad. The Engineers were small. But they had plenty of spirit and they looked lightning fast. "They've got the speed," Chip muttered.

A few minutes later, the horn sounded, and the teams lined up for the jump ball at center court. Then all the lights except those illuminating the court were dimmed, and Chip was gripped by that empty, hollow-chested, wobbly-legged feeling that overwhelms most athletes just before the opening play of a game.

Coach Corrigan started the same team that had defeated mighty Southwestern in the finals of the Holiday Invitational Tournament. Sky Bollinger got the tap, and immediately Tech showed its hand. Each player moved rapidly out on the defense to meet his assigned opponent, sticking to him like glue, pressing and forcing him constantly back.

Soapy elbowed Chip in the ribs. "This is the first time I ever saw you in the stands. Now you'll learn how a fan feels about the game."

Chip found out about that quick enough. He found himself fighting and straining for every rebound and loose ball and suffering and yelling when Tech scored. There wasn't much basketball being played down on the court. The game had developed into a wild, rushing, running, tumbling, up-and-down-the-court melee; it was basketball in name only. After five minutes of action, Tech led, 14-6.

"C'mon, c'mon!" Soapy yelled, shoving and pushing and thumping Chip on the back. "Get the ball! What's the matter with you guys? Look at that!"

Coach Corrigan had sent his team out on the floor with instructions to use the same zone press that had been so successful in the tournament. Surprisingly, the Tech coach had retaliated with the same strategy. The Engineers were agile and fired up, and they pursued the ball as if they were tied to it with an invisible string. They followed in every shot, double-teaming State's rebounders as soon as they got the ball, advancing furiously with a wild abandon that forced bad passes and resulted in frequent interceptions. Neither team presented a set pattern of attack or defense. There was no retreat and no letup.

Coach Corrigan, always wanting his team to play through difficult stretches, finally had to take a time-out. The State players, with sweat pouring off their faces, circled him with their arms on each other's shoulders. They all glanced uneasily at the scoreboard. Chip could almost hear them saying, "What happened? What happened?"

Corrigan was talking excitedly, and Chip could tell by his gestures that he was trying to get the team to settle down. Then he tapped Bill King and Bradley Gowdy, and they ran to the scorers' table to report. Sky Bollinger and Bitsy Reardon pulled their warm-up jackets over their shoulders and slumped down on the bench. The horn blared, and both teams promptly resumed the mad, continuous scramble, no holds barred.

The three officials were doing their best to keep up with the fast pace, but it was impossible. When a foul was committed, the whistle was far behind the play. The boos of the fans who missed the infractions added to the tumult. At the half Tech led, 61-54. State's celebrated zone press had backfired.

The second half was a duplication of the first. The fans shrieked, yelled, whistled, cheered, and stamped their feet. They pushed, jostled, elbowed, and swayed with each shot. The State band got into the game with loud blasts from the horns and booming of drums, and the cheerleaders from both schools made vain efforts to initiate organized cheers.

"Jimmy will have to do it, Soapy," Chip said, glancing worriedly at the scoreboard.

"Somebody better do it," Soapy moaned.

Tech led 77-61 when Jimmy Chung tried to take control of the game, which he had done so successfully against Southwestern. But Bob O'Brien, Tech's wily coach, had assigned a small, speedy guard to play the clever ball handler. And this defender fell for none of the master dribbler's fakes. He played Jimmy loose and let him dribble all over the court until he tried for an opening to the basket.

"It won't work," Chip breathed. "We've got to have points."

"Yeah," Soapy agreed. "We'd better go back to the press."

Chip nodded. "That's all that will keep us in the game."

State had abandoned the dribbling strategy now, and the press resulted in a lot of interceptions. But State couldn't quite catch up. Tech always managed to keep ahead. With two minutes to go, the Engineers led by four, 109-105. Then the game got completely out of hand.

A Tech player stabbed at the ball and knocked it out of Jimmy's hand, and practically every player on the court dove for the recovery. When the officials untangled the scrambling mob of players, Jimmy and his opponent got up swinging. It took the combined efforts of the officials and both coaches to separate the players. Coach Corrigan promptly removed Chung, Bill King, and Bradley Gowdy and substituted Speed Morris, Rudy Slater, and Dom Di Santis.

Both benches were on edge now, and it showed in the players' angry, set faces. Out on the court, they scrambled and dove for the ball. It was worse than street basketball, almost more like football! The players, desperately attempting to gain or keep the ball, spilled wildly across the floor, and all the time the minutes and seconds on the game clock clicked down toward 00:00.

Chip was yelling at the top of his voice, but the sound was lost in the continuous roar of the crowd. "Come on, guys. Get the ball! You've got to score!"

But it was too late. The Tech players fought grimly to hold the lead, and the wild contest ended with players of both teams sprawled all over the court. The final score: Tech 111, State 107. The Engineers had upset the tournament champions.

Chip glanced gloomily at Soapy and slumped back down in his seat. Soapy hunched over, and the two friends sat there without speaking while the fans filed down the steps. When the section had completely emptied, they made their way slowly down the aisle to the mezzanine. The exit there was clogged by fans packed close together, slowly trudging along. Chip and Soapy sat down in two empty seats to wait for the crowd to clear.

Most of the Tech fans had managed to beat the rush. But a few were caught behind with the slower-moving State fans. Chip and Soapy listened to the crowd's remarks.

"Corrigan lost the game," a man dressed in State's red, blue, and white said angrily. "He took King, Chung, and Gowdy out just when we had a run going."

"Right! The officials didn't put 'em out. Corrigan did!"

"You didn't see Bob O'Brien pulling any of *his* players out of the game."

"Aw, what are you griping about?" a hostile voice yelled. "Can't you take it?"

"We can take it. And we'll take Tech the next time!"

"You got that right!" a State supporter added. "Tech was lucky tonight. Half our team is injured."

"You mean Hilton?"

"That's right!"

"Wouldn't have made any difference tonight. Tech was red-hot!"

Chip was leaning on the back of the seat in front of him and looking down at the court. He didn't see the writers who were busily typing away on their laptops to record the story of the upset; Chip was thinking about the game and how badly his teammates must be feeling at that moment. He squared his jaw and gripped his knee. Maybe he could play against Midwestern.

SOAPED AGAIN!

Soapy jogged Chip's elbow. "There's Locke," he said, nodding toward the reporter still seated at the scorers' table. "He's grinning. Looks like Sylvester the cat when he swallows Tweety Bird. Wonder what's going on in that poisonous mind? Bad news for someone."

CHAPTER 3

The College Hoopla Show

SOAPY SMITH glanced at his sleeping roommate and slipped quietly out of bed. He threw on jeans and headed downstairs to grab a paper from the stack that was delivered early every morning to the front porch of Jefferson Hall. When he returned, Chip was sitting in front of his computer, about to check his E-mail.

"What did I tell you last night?" Soapy said excitedly, waving a copy of the *News* in the air. "What did I tell you about Locke?"

"Bad?" Chip asked as he yawned and rubbed his eyes.

Soapy nodded and flicked the paper with his index finger. "Listen to this headline. Quote: 'Tech surprises State. State athletic brass responsible for Tech upset.'

"How's that for openers? Now get this: 'State's tournament champions were upset last night because of an antiquated schedule-making policy that is designed to ensure State teams of easy victories against nonconference schools—'"

"Nonconference schools!" Chip blurted. "Most of them are tougher than the league teams!"

"That's what it says. Listen! 'The defeat may teach the State schedule architects a lesson. To wit: Big schools should play in their own class and forgo the development of synthetic victory records at the expense of small-school setups.'"

"Some setup," Chip said. "They nearly ran us out of the gym."

Soapy nodded and continued reading. "'Tech caught the Statesmen asleep, overconfident, and unprepared and scored an unexpected 111-107 win. It was the Engineers' eighth-consecutive victory of the season. With the exception of last night's win, Tech has met only second-class competition.'"

Soapy paused and eyed Chip expectantly. "What do you think of that?"

"It isn't very kind to Tech."

"*Kind?* Locke doesn't know the meaning of the word."

"Doesn't he say anything about the game?"

"Plenty! He says there was a big fight near the end and that three State players were sent out of the game."

"But that's not true!" Chip protested. "Coach took them out himself. They weren't ejected at all."

"Of course they weren't! The torch of truth means about as much to Locke as a secondhand toothpick. That reminds me, I'm hungry. And we're going to be late if we don't get moving."

Chip had to force his pace to make the first class. There had been a lot of days during his freshman year and this year, too, when he had felt like skipping a class—days when the bruising knocks of a tough scrimmage or a rough game had left protesting muscles and aching bones. But Chip had come to State with two great ambitions, and he wasn't going to let a little physical discomfort interfere. First, he was determined to get a good education. Second, he was resolved to take advantage of all the expert coaching State's athletic staff provided. And from his very first day at State, Chip had permitted nothing short of absolute sickness to sidetrack his plans and dreams. It wasn't always easy, but it was right.

Chip's path to a college education was not an easy one, but it was the path he had chosen, and he was making it happen. That was rewarding too. In his junior and senior years at Valley Falls High School, colleges had actively recruited Chip and several had offered him athletic scholarships. He was flattered to receive such attention and so many offers.

He and his mom, Mary Hilton, had talked it all over, the way they did just about everything that was important to either of them. They finally reached their decision. Chip asked Henry Rockwell, longtime family friend and coach, to tell all the recruiters Chip had decided he was going to State University just as his dad, "Big Chip" Hilton, had done years before. And he wanted to pay his own way. Chip and his mom had put away all the money they could from her small savings and Chip's after-school job at the Sugar Bowl back home in Valley Falls. Most of Mary Hilton's salary with the phone company was needed to maintain the family home, so Chip was pretty much on his own, and he was proud of it. Fortunately, his experience during high school at the Sugar Bowl had qualified him for the stockroom job at Grayson's. So far, he was doing all right.

State's students were not exactly in mourning following the Tech defeat, but they were hurt. Bad! It was a shock. They had dropped from the heights of elation to the dregs of disappointment in one fell swoop. But the unexpected loss did not dampen their support for the team. They greeted the players warmly, and Chip was thrilled by their loyalty.

"Tough loss, Hilton. Too bad you couldn't play."

"Yeah. Things would have been different."

"Hey, Chip, get well quick! We need you!"

His classmates' loyalty filled Chip with the determination to prove his appreciation. "I'll make up for it," he vowed, "one way or another."

Chip and his Valley Falls friends met together every day for lunch unless a class interfered. Their regular meeting place was a good-sized table in a corner of the cafeteria in the student union. Today they were all there: Soapy, Speed, Biggie Cohen, and Red Schwartz were waiting when Chip arrived. At an adjoining table Fireball Finley, Whitty Whittemore, and Jimmy Chung were discussing the game.

"Hey, Chip," Jimmy said glumly. "Not so good, huh?"

"You can't win them all, Jimmy."

"I don't mean that; I mean the fight. If you could even call it a fight. I guess I haven't learned much about sportsmanship."

"Nonsense."

"It's not nonsense," Jimmy said earnestly. "I'll never know why I lost my head last night. And right in front of everybody in school. I'm a jerk."

"You weren't the only one," Fireball said. "How about King and Gowdy?"

"They haven't got the slightest thing to do with it. I lost the game."

"Knock it off!" Speed growled, looking up from his spaghetti. "Basketball's a team game. We lost it."

"You guys read Locke's column this morning?" Fireball asked, obviously attempting to change the subject.

"Some difference between Locke and Bill Bell," Soapy said, pulling a copy of the *Herald* out of his pocket. "Bell says we were overconfident. Gives Corrigan a good plug for sportsmanship too."

"I haven't seen Bill Bell's column," Speed added significantly, "but I'll bet *he* didn't call Tech a small-school setup."

"Right," Soapy agreed. "Bell says the athletic program at Tech is outstanding. No undue emphasis is placed on representative teams, but the school recognizes the value of competitive sports—"

"Here, here!" Speed interrupted. "You memorize that, man?"

"And," Soapy continued glibly, "he says it's too bad Tech's present basketball team isn't playing a big-time schedule, because it's a big-time team. Furthermore, gentlemen, Mr. Bell says the local rivalry is good and should be exploited to the fullest extent."

"I always wondered who *really* wrote Bill Bell's column. You doing some ghostwriting, Soapy?" Whitty asked pointedly.

Soapy cleared his throat. "Ahem . . . er . . . thanks, Mr. Whitty." He rose to his feet. "Well, gentlemen, ahem . . . I regret that Mr. Hilton and I have been assigned an extremely exhaustive and demanding schedule by our respective collegiate advisers at State University. And, much as it grieves us, we must leave." He turned to Chip. "Shall we drop in on Professor Reid and initiate our survey?"

"We certainly should," Chip said, grinning. "Especially since he's expecting us."

Chip's science lab lasted until four o'clock, and practice was well underway when he reached the gym. He found Murph Kelly alone in the locker room. The experienced trainer went right to work on his knee.

"Coach says you're not to go on the trip, Hilton. Says you're to rest until we get back."

"You sure? I feel fine."

"Of course I'm sure. Coach's orders. Oh, I'm supposed to tell you Coach wants you to appear on Bill Bell's show. Bell's gonna pick you up here at five o'clock."

"Oh, no!"

"Don't blame me. I'm just the messenger. Coach's orders."

Chip moaned in disgust. "Why me, Murph?"

"Because Bill Bell wants you. That's why."

"But it's not fair to the other players."

"Stop being temperamental. Sportswriters are important people, and sports need publicity. All kinds. Besides, the show isn't just about sports; it's about college life. I'm pretty sure Bell will focus on basketball with you though."

Kelly was still lecturing when Bill Bell knocked on the door. He entered and stood framed in the open door. "Hi ya, Murph. Hello, Chip. Guess we timed it about right."

As Bell drove Chip to the local TV station near the *Herald* building, he quizzed him about his knee and then switched to the marksmanship tournament. "I sure hope your knee comes along, Chip. You're pretty important to the marksmanship tournament. This year, we're going to have our biggest entry in the history of the event. Now about the program this evening—the show is done live, and there's a small studio audience. The producers will mail you a tape of the show. It's kind of our custom around here; we give each of our guests a copy."

HARDCOURT UPSET

On the set, Bell sat down and motioned Chip to a chair beside him. While waiting for the crew to finish setting things up, Bell leafed through some notes. A minute or so later, two cameramen maneuvered their cameras in front of them. A director followed, motioning for silence. Bill Bell smiled at Chip and faced the lens. Then a red spot glowed on the close-up camera, and the director nodded his head.

"Good evening, everyone. I'm your host, Bill Bell. Welcome once again to the 'College Hoopla Show.' As you know, our program is dedicated to presenting the best in collegiate life on and off the playing fields." When he finished, he winked at Chip. "And now I want to present a special guest, State University's William 'Chip' Hilton—"

The red eye of the camera focused on Chip as Bell introduced him.

"This young man, a Dean's List student, has made sports history in the year and a half he has been a student at State. He starred in three sports as a freshman as part of the Freshmen Pilot Program and won the AAU basketball marksmanship title. This past fall he piloted Coach Curly Ralston's varsity football team so brilliantly that he won all-American honors as State's quarterback. Then, switching to basketball, he sparked State's hoop team to the Holiday Invitational Tournament championship and was voted the Most Valuable Player."

Bell then questioned Chip about his knee and the extent of the injury and followed this by switching to the Tech game. "This is a difficult question, Chip—probably painful, too—but what was *your* reaction to the big upset of your teammates last night? Was it a letdown after the big victory at Springfield?"

"I don't believe so, Mr. Bell."

"You don't think they underestimated Tech?"

Chip smiled. "If they did, it was only for about two minutes."

"There's no question about that. Now what's your opinion of the Tech players?"

"All the Tech players are fine shooters, Mr. Bell, and they can really move. They also play well as a team."

"Should the team be ranked nationally?"

"Yes. Absolutely. It's one of the best teams I have seen this year."

"How do you think they would have made out in the tournament? Could they have given, say, Southwestern a good game?"

"I think so, sir. Playing as they did last night, they would have beaten any team."

"One last question, Chip. Do you think small schools, small colleges like Tech, should have the opportunity to compete for the national championship?"

"I think all colleges, large or small, should have the opportunity to compete for the national championship. Naturally it matters what division those schools are in— but I think that should be up to the school—based on the NCAA guidelines and rules, of course.

"March Madness pumps everybody up! It's even more exciting when a small 'Cinderella' school upsets a big powerhouse and makes a run at the national championship. The size of the student body isn't what I see as being important. It's the team on the floor that matters. I think Tech is a good example. The college is small, but the team is great."

"I'm glad to hear you say that." Bill Bell smiled as the camera moved toward him. "It also takes real sportsmanship to praise a rival after a bitter defeat. Well, I see that it's time to take questions from our audience, and we've got some callers on the line also wanting to talk to you. I know they join me in wishing you a quick recovery and an early return to the State basketball team. I don't have to add that the *Herald* and the marksmanship selection committee members are anxious to see if you will be the first champion to win the title two years in succession.

"Here's our first question from the audience . . ."

Thousands of loyal fans either watched or heard about Bill Bell's program that evening. In Valley Falls, Chip's hometown, The "College Hoopla Show" was especially popular that evening. Doc Jones, his pal John Schroeder, Mary Hilton, Petey Jackson, and hundreds of Chip's friends watched and were happy for him.

Jim Locke had also tuned in. He liked to pick up material directly from his bitter rival's show—especially when it focused on sports.

Locke grinned scornfully, clicked off his TV remote, and, as if suddenly inspired, sat at his desk and turned on his computer. "This gets more interesting all the time," he muttered aloud.

CHAPTER 4

The Best Interests of His Athletes

SOAPY SMITH was angry after reading Locke's column the next morning. "There oughta be a law, Chip," he said darkly, pacing back and forth in front of his bed.

"Why? What about?" Chip asked as he grabbed two books from the shelf over his desk and shoved them into his backpack.

"To take care of guys like this armchair sports expert. Listen—"

"I can't, Soapy. I'm late." Chip hurried away, trying to keep from limping and anxious to escape Soapy's tirade. But when he joined his friends in the student union for lunch, there was no escape.

"What are you going to do about it?" Soapy demanded.

"About what?" Chip parried.

"About Locke. He slammed Bill Bell and you in his column this morning. Said you were Bell's yes man."

"So what?"

"So what? Are you going to take that?"

"Sure. What else can I do?"

"You can punch him in the nose!" Soapy exclaimed.

"Sure," Chip agreed calmly, "that would be good. I'd end up getting thrown out of school. Then he *would* have the right to spout off in his column. Nothing doing."

"But, Chip, he implied you're on Bell's marksmanship tournament payroll too," Whitty added, a deep frown running across his forehead. "That could get you into trouble."

"Not when it isn't true," Chip said softly. "Everyone knows the AAU runs the tournament and that every penny is accounted for and published in the papers. No one would believe Locke about that."

"Why pick on you?" Fireball mused.

"Maybe it's because I agree with Mr. Bell that Tech is a first-rate team."

"That's it," Jimmy said quickly. "Locke isn't after Chip; he's feuding with Bill Bell. He goes after anyone who's on Bell's side. He's been fighting with Bell for years, or trying to."

"I didn't want to go on that TV show," Chip said ruefully, "but Murph said it was Coach's orders. No more of that for me."

"Let's forget it," Fireball suggested. "My high school coach used to say he was happy when he got his name on the sports pages, whether he was getting heat or praise. You going with the team this afternoon, Chip?"

"No. I'd just take up space. Anyway, Murph has enough to do on a road trip without taking care of me. Two games in two days is tough. Well, I've got to head to class. Good luck, Speed, Jimmy. You can take 'em!"

But Speed, Jimmy, and their teammates couldn't "take 'em." Midwestern defeated State, 84-80. Chip and

THE BEST INTEREST OF HIS ATHLETES

Soapy caught parts of the game on the big-screen TV at Grayson's in between customers and inventory. After the loss, they didn't even stop at Pete's Place after work for their usual nightly snack.

Saturday was cold and rainy, and business at Grayson's was slow all morning. Late that afternoon, when State faced Western, gloom settled on the store like a black London fog. The Statesmen lost their third game in a row that afternoon at Western, 91-90.

Chip was so despondent that he again passed up the after-work gathering at Pete's Place. It was raining so steadily he was glad to let Soapy drive him home in Mitzi's car. "Oh, man," Soapy cried, looking at the gauge on the dashboard, "we're on empty! I don't know why Mitzi runs this thing practically dry all the time."

"Well, we better get some gas," Chip said. "I sure don't want to walk to Jeff in this stuff."

Soapy's eyes searched for the closest station. "There's a place on the left, and they've got a full-service pump. I'm not getting out in this either."

It was a downpour when they pulled into the Triangle Mini Mart for gas. The rain was beating down on the windshield and windows so heavily that Chip could scarcely see the face of the attendant who reluctantly approached the car.

"You *would* come now," the man growled, shielding his eyeglasses with his hand and peering at Soapy through the open window. "Fill 'er up?"

"No way. Sorry, buddy, just two dollars' worth," Soapy said sympathetically, extending two soggy one-dollar bills.

The man pursed his lips and glared angrily at Soapy. "Humph!" he snarled in disgust. "Another smart college kid. Humph! Two dollars' worth! And in all this rain!"

It was a bad night to drive, and Chip was relieved when they reached Jeff and he could go to bed. But he couldn't get to sleep. And when Soapy returned, they talked a long time in the dark about the quick disaster that had overtaken the team.

Sunday dawned clear and cold. Chip awoke at daylight and glanced out the window. Then he sighed contentedly and pulled the blankets up under his chin. *This is the life,* he was thinking. Now for a good, long snooze. No school and no need to get up until it was time to go to church. It seemed only a second later when Soapy shook him awake. "Hey, Chip! Wake up!"

Chip looked at the redhead in amazement. "What's wrong with you?" he demanded. "This is my morning to sleep late, remember?"

"I know, I know, Chip," Soapy apologized. "It's the bus."

"Bus? What bus?"

"At nine thirty. The bus the team is coming in on."

"What about it?"

"Well, the team lost and—"

Chip stopped him and grinned. "You're right! Good idea! I'll be dressed in a second."

"But your knee . . ."

"Don't worry. I'll be all right."

Soapy shook his head worriedly. "I didn't expect you to go, Chip. I just needed a little help."

"What kind of help?"

"Well, you're president of Jeff hall, right? So, if you say the word, everybody goes! Right?"

"Right! Pass the word."

Soapy passed the word. His banging on every door brought students out of each room. "Pass the word!" Soapy shouted. "Chip's orders! Everybody meets the basketball team at Assembly Hall at 9:30. See you there!"

THE BEST INTEREST OF HIS ATHLETES

Soapy and a group of guys from Jeff were waiting for Chip in one of the guy's cars, and just as they pulled out of the lot, more and more of Jeff's residents came streaming down the walk, falling enthusiastically in line to show their support of the team.

Thirty minutes later, the bus carrying State's varsity hoop team pulled up in front of Assembly Hall. The players stared in disbelief at the crowd lining the walkway and practically blocking the drive. But only for a second. Soapy leaped up on some of his fellow Jeffs' shoulders and started the cheers.

"Yea, team! Yea, State! Who do we appreciate?"

"Corrigan!" Chip yelled.

"Corrigan!" the guys cheered. "Corrigan!"

"Say it again!" Soapy yelled.

"Corrigan!"

And so it went. Right down the line from Coach Jim Corrigan to his assistant, Henry Rockwell, to co-captains Kirk Barkley and Andy Thornhill, to Bill King, Jimmy Chung, Speed Morris, and all the other players, with a last big cheer for Murph Kelly and his assistant trainers.

Then the rally broke up. The players grabbed their bags from the bus's underbelly and headed through the doors leading into their hallowed basketball home, Assembly Hall, their weariness and dejection blasted away by Jeff's loyal ovation.

The last to enter, Jim Corrigan and Henry Rockwell stood on the sidewalk and watched as the caravan of cars wound down the drive and streamed away up University Boulevard. Corrigan sighed deeply. "Kids are great, Rock. Makes me feel wonderful when I see a bunch of kids do something so spontaneous and real as this little rally."

"I've been feeling that way for thirty-nine years, Jim."

"Maybe coaching isn't so tough after all," Corrigan said softly.

The young coach and the veteran stood side by side, impervious to the cold, steeped in thought. Corrigan broke the silence. "Say, Rock, we ought to do something for Smith. I've never felt he had a fair chance to make the squad."

"You had to cut someone, Jim. Soapy didn't have time to get adjusted after football, that's all. Chip and Speed are natural athletes. Soapy has to pay a bigger price for everything he does. But I suspect he'll be more prepared when the season rolls around next time, and he'll probably have had some help from his Valley Falls friends."

Corrigan nodded. "I guess you're right, but it seems a shame about this season. I never knew an athlete with more enthusiasm."

"Or more loyalty," Rockwell added. "Well, we're home. Let's go in."

Later that morning, huddled around a table at Pete's Place, the guys discussed the two defeats.

"What happened?" Soapy asked.

"They were too good for us, that's all," Speed said ruefully.

Jimmy nodded in agreement. "Right! We fought, all right, both games. But we've got to face it. Without Chip, we haven't got a scoring punch."

"That's not true," Chip interrupted. "You beat the greatest team in the country with me on the bench."

"Sure," Jimmy agreed. "But we surprised them with our zone press. Now everybody's ready for it."

"Tech set the pattern, Chip," Speed said. "Coach O'Brien scouted us at Springfield and saw the difference our press makes, and he got Tech ready for it. The other teams are ready now too. And without you to give us thirty or forty points a game, we haven't got a chance. Especially against the *good* teams."

"I'm not sure I believe—" Chip began.

"Believe it!" Soapy cut in. "It's true. No team can afford to lose a thirty-point player."

"He's so right, Chip, my man," Speed said earnestly. "I sure hope you can play Wednesday night. If we lose to Cathedral, we might as well turn in our uniforms. They haven't won a game all year."

"Think you can play, Chip?" Jimmy asked.

Chip nodded. "I'll play."

Chip's decision to get back into action was strengthened further that afternoon. As he was leaving church, he shook hands with Pastor Potts, as he always did, and the minister smiled. "We're sure counting on you to get well and back out on the court, son." And then, on his way home, several people he didn't know came up to ask him about his knee. Seemed as if wherever he went, everyone was interested in finding out when he would be back in the lineup. When he reached Jeff, he found the *News* and the *Herald* opened to the sports pages.

Halfway down Jim Locke's column in the *News,* Soapy had highlighted a phrase: "What is wrong with Chip Hilton? Is the brilliant scoring star resting on his tournament laurels?"

That hit home, but Chip felt a little better after reading the *Herald.* Soapy had underlined a couple of phrases in Bill Bell's column too. Chip breathed a little easier as he read the first one. "The Statesmen's third-consecutive loss serves to reiterate my previous statement that Chip Hilton is irreplaceable and of vital importance to Jim Corrigan's team."

"I wish he'd stop writing that stuff," Chip murmured. Then he read the other paragraph Soapy had marked. "I talked to Coach Jim Corrigan early this morning about his star scorer, and I would like to quote his reply: 'We need Chip Hilton badly, but no basketball victory or basketball season is important enough to warrant the use of an athlete as long as there is any chance of worsening an injury.' . . . That reply, fans, marks Coach Jim Corrigan as a fine coach with the best interests of his athletes coming first."

"You can say that again," Chip said aloud.

Chip took a long walk that afternoon to limber up his knee and spent the rest of the day studying and working on several drafts of his history paper.

All day Monday—at the Student Union, in his classes, and just about everywhere on the campus—Chip's classmates and friends asked about his knee. But behind their interest, Chip could sense they wanted him to return to the team.

"You're walking OK, Hilton. Couldn't you give it a try?"

"What does Doc Terring say?"

"I thought for sure we would win the conference this year."

Chip reported for practice that afternoon determined to play. But he ran into trouble. Murph Kelly was sympathetic but unyielding. "Work out? Nothing doing! Not until Doc gives me an OK. Forget what people say!"

"Can I see Dr. Terring today?"

"Nope," Kelly said shortly. "Maybe tomorrow. Not before."

Chip's jaw firmed, and for a second an angry retort formed in his mind. But he said nothing. Murph Kelly was his friend, and he couldn't be angry with someone who was trying to help him. "All right, Murph," he said. "I'll wait, but I think I'm ready."

Tuesday was a rough day. Chip caught pressure from every side. The only encouraging event was the new brace Dr. Terring had for him. It fit his knee like a glove. "Oh, yes!" Chip exulted. "I can do it. I can play."

Later that day, when the action at Grayson's tapered off around 8:30, Chip decided to give his mom a call in Valley Falls. When she answered the phone, Chip explained that he had a new brace.

"It's a perfect fit, Mom, and it gives me a lot of support," he explained.

"You said the doctor gave you a new brace, but how's your knee, Chip?" Mrs. Hilton remonstrated. "What about that?"

"I've got to play, Mom. I'm on the spot."

"You still haven't said anything about your knee. When are you going to see Dr. Terring again?"

"Tomorrow afternoon."

"Well, Chip, if he says you can play, all right. But if it means a lot of pain . . ."

"Don't worry, Mom. If Doc Terring gives me permission to play against Cathedral, I'll be able to stand the pain!"

CHAPTER 5

On Empty Again!

DR. MIKE TERRING, an avid sports enthusiast, liked his job as State University's team physician, which was in addition to his private practice. But the task confronting him this particular afternoon was extremely distasteful. Terring keenly recognized Chip's importance to State's basketball team, and he also realized the emotional factors involved. But Dr. Terring was, first and always foremost, a physician. He eyed Chip, shrugged his broad shoulders, and turned to Murph Kelly. "What do you think, Murph?"

"He's moving pretty good, Doc," Kelly said. "And the new brace—"

"I wanted to ask you about that," Terring interrupted.

"It's great, Doc," Chip responded. "It gives me plenty of support, and I'm sure I can play."

Dr. Terring hesitated. "Well," he said reluctantly, "if Murph puts a good bandage under the brace, I don't see how you can do much damage."

ON EMPTY AGAIN!

He looked at the trainer questioningly.

Kelly nodded and turned away, muttering something unintelligible. Chip followed jubilantly and started for home, eager to tell his friends the good news. But when he reached the door, he stopped in dismay. A storm was blowing, and wild gusts of wind sprayed cold sleet in every direction.

It took him half an hour to cover a distance that usually required less than ten minutes. When he reached Jeff, his leg was cold and tired. Speed was studying in the library room on the first floor and saw Chip come in. He rushed into the hall. "Where have you been? You crazy? Why didn't you call me or borrow the car?"

Chip explained the result of his visit to Dr. Terring. As soon as Speed heard the good news, he headed for the phone. "You get some rest," he called over his shoulder. "I'm going to call Soapy."

It was 6:30 when Soapy appeared with sub sandwiches and milk shakes. The redhead was excited and happy. "Oh, baby! Things will be different now! Wish I could see it. Look! Mitzi told me to drive you guys to the game and then hurry back to work. But she said I was to come back for you at 10:30."

Speed gave Soapy a long look. "I've got wheels. What do you need Mitzi's car for?"

When Soapy stammered and looked down at the floor, a look of comprehension spread across Speed's face, and he laughed. "OK, I see where this thing is headed. Love is a many splendored thing, right, Soapy?"

By the time Soapy drove Chip and Speed to Assembly Hall, the sleet had changed to a wet snow. "That's a help," Soapy said gratefully. "Looked as if we were in for a real ice storm. You guys kill 'em, and I'll be back for you at 10:30."

Murph Kelly had alerted Chip's teammates that he had been cleared to play, and they let him have it as soon as he opened the door.

"All right, Chipper!"

"We'll get 'em now!"

"This is the best news since the tournament!"

Coach Corrigan and Henry Rockwell came in while Kelly was bandaging Chip's knee, and they examined the brace carefully. "Go through the warm-ups slowly, Chip," Coach Corrigan said. "I may not use you, but I want to be sure you're OK just in case." He turned to the board and sketched several diagrams. "All right, men, give me your attention."

It was a disagreeable night, but surprisingly a good crowd turned out for the game. When State ran out on the floor, the loyal fans gave their team a rousing reception. When they realized Chip was back in uniform, the applause increased dramatically. The fans watched every move he made, hoping he was back in shape. But the brace restricted free use of his knee, and it was easy to see that his movements were awkward.

Chip's shooting eye was still on the beam, and his shots began dropping through the hoop from all angles. Then the horn cut through the noise of the crowd, and the game was on.

State led from the opening toss, and the score at the half was State 39, Cathedral 34. Corrigan made no move to use Chip during this period because the Statesmen seemed to have the game well under control. But in the second half, Cathedral racked up three quick baskets and took the lead, 40-39.

Barkley called time, and the fans began to chant: "We want Hilton! We want Hilton!"

Corrigan glanced at Chip uncertainly, but Murph

ON EMPTY AGAIN!

Kelly murmured something in the coach's ear, and the same team went back into the game. Cathedral kept right on going, and with the score 47-43 in favor of the visitors, Corrigan called for a time-out. There were thirteen minutes left to play, and the fans began chanting in unison over and over: "We want Hilton! We want Hilton!"

Corrigan shook his head grimly and turned to the bench. "All right, Chip. Give it a whirl. But let me know if it's no go. No hero stuff."

"I'll be all right, Coach," Chip said, adding a fervent "I hope," under his breath.

Chip joined teammate Andy Thornhill at forward and Sky Bollinger at center as Speed Morris and Jimmy Chung brought the ball up the floor. Chip assessed the combination and breathed a sigh of relief. Speed and Jimmy could do the cutting, and he could handle the ball and set up the plays. But it didn't work out that way.

Speed and Chip had played on the same teams for years, and Speed knew how to set his friend's favorite screens to shoot over. He also knew the fast-moving clear-outs and the give-and-go plays that gave Chip room for his shots. And they worked! Speed set up four straight shots, and Chip hit for three. During this time, Cathedral scored only once. Chip's third basket tied the score.

Then Jimmy Chung got the idea, and he, too, began to set Chip up for the long shots from the corner. The crowd was in an uproar as State and Cathedral matched baskets right down the stretch. Chip felt little pain, but the brace hampered his starts and stops, and it was impossible for him to muster enough speed for a drive. So he concentrated on his passing to teammates and his jump shots. With thirty seconds to play, the score was tied, 81-81, and State had the ball. Andy Thornhill got

Corrigan's sign for a time-out, and the team circled the coach in front of the State bench.

"Let Jimmy hold it for one shot," Coach Corrigan said decisively. "You take it out of bounds, Chip, and pass to Jimmy. Speed, you set the pick. The rest of you cut toward the basket but don't charge anyone. Got it? OK. Let's go!"

Chip took the ball out of bounds at midcourt. When time was in, Speed set a pick for Jimmy in the outer half of the free-throw circle, and Chip hit the little dribbler with a perfect pass at the head of the circle.

Jimmy dribbled slowly to the right and glanced at the clock. Then he began his dribble to run some time off the shot clock. Chip and Speed opened up the backcourt, and Sky Bollinger and Andy Thornhill went to the baseline corners. Jimmy froze the ball all by himself, dribbling with such uncanny skill that it looked as easy as controlling a yo-yo. As the little spark plug played out the clock and kept control of the ball for the last shot, the applause of the home fans grew and grew in wild acclaim.

When the game clock showed fifteen seconds left in the game, Jimmy began to maneuver for position. His opponent now knew what to expect and kept as far away as possible without giving Jimmy too much room for his patented quick drive to the hoop. But he underestimated Jimmy's feinting ability. Jimmy faked right, left, and then sped to the right, gaining a half-step lead on his guard. At the free-throw line he leaped high in the air and thrust the ball over his head for a jump shot.

Then Sky Bollinger's tall opponent made a mistake; he thought it was the real final shot and switched to block the ball. Jimmy faked the shot with his empty right hand and deftly zipped the ball to Sky with a cross-arm bounce pass. Bollinger was all alone when he dunked the ball through the hoop to win the game, 83-81.

Chip's leg ached, but he was happy. After his shower, he waited until the trainer finished with the other players. Then Kelly gave his knee a short ice treatment and bandaged it tightly. "You can loosen the bandage when you go to bed," he said when Chip protested. "Personally, I think you were a fool to play tonight. If I had my way, you would turn in your uniform right now."

Kelly turned abruptly away, but as Chip and Speed were leaving, he growled, "Good night."

When Chip and Speed pushed through the front doors, the storm was in full swing. Through the darkness in the nearly empty parking lot, they saw Mitzi's car, with Soapy at the wheel flashing the headlights. They hurried toward the car, and Soapy and the warm interior were welcoming. "Nice going, guys," Soapy cried. "Now we're back on the victory train." He reached back and patted Chip's knee. "Hear you got sixteen points, Chipper. Great! Your leg OK?"

"Never mind my leg. You be careful with this car. It's a bad night, and the roads are slick."

Soapy dropped his two buddies off at Jeff and started back to Grayson's. Just as he turned off the campus, he noticed a red flashing light on the dash. It was the fuel indicator! "Oh, no," he muttered to himself. "She's done it again! Doesn't Mitzi *ever* put any gas in this thing?"

Just ahead, the lights of the Triangle Mini Mart streamed across the street, and Soapy drove to the self-service pump. He turned off the motor and was out of the car before the engine stopped, frantically searching through the pockets of his jeans. "Seventy cents!" he moaned. Ducking back into the car, Soapy looked through the console, between the seats, and on the floor.

His search produced an additional seventy-seven cents, which he jammed into his jeans pocket. He pumped the gas and went inside.

"What?" the same old man asked sharply.

"I said I was on pump number one and that I got $1.47 worth," Soapy said in a muffled voice, embarrassed again as he searched each one of his pockets for more money before taking off his soaking baseball cap and nervously ruffling his red hair. His cheeks were bright red, and a drop of melting snow hung stubbornly from the tip of his nose.

"A big spender, ain't you? I'll bet you're either that Bill Gates computer fella or one of those smart college students. Humph! And would you look at the floor! Kid, you're dripping wet! I just mopped that floor, and now you've gone and puddled it all up!"

The man placed the quarters, dimes, nickels, and pennies Soapy sheepishly offered into their respective slots and then slammed the cash register drawer closed, all the while muttering under his breath. He was grabbing his mop and bucket again when Soapy pulled out of the station.

Soapy drove slowly and carefully down Main Street. A block from Grayson's, he recognized Jennifer Andrews, one of the newest Grayson's employees, standing all alone at the bus shelter. Soapy pulled to the curb and opened the car door. "Hey!" he called. "Jennifer! It's me! Soapy. Hop in. I'll drive you home."

Jennifer peered in at Soapy and then ducked into the car. "What a night!" she gasped, shivering. "I'm nearly frozen. I've been standing on that corner since 10:30. My mom will be worried sick."

"What time is it now?"

"It can't be five after eleven," Jennifer said in disgust,

pointing to the dash clock. Soapy switched on the interior light, and Jennifer checked her wristwatch. "Exactly right. It would be, knowing Mitzi. Someone ought to do something about the bus service in this town."

The car passed Grayson's at that moment. Soapy cast an agonized glance through the window. The store was practically empty. "Oh, oh," he whispered frantically. "I'm in trouble. I'll never make it."

"What did you say?" Jennifer asked.

"Where do you live? How far is it?"

"About twenty minutes. A little longer, maybe, on a night like this."

The car leaped forward as Soapy pushed down on the accelerator, the wheels spinning and screeching before they got traction.

"Be careful!" Jennifer gasped. "You're driving Mitzi's car, remember."

"You're telling me," Soapy groaned, glancing at the ever-thirsty gas gauge.

It was exactly twenty-five minutes after eleven when Soapy pulled up in front of Jennifer's house. "You sure drive fast," Jennifer said. "Exactly twenty minutes. Good night, Soapy, and thanks a million."

Soapy waited impatiently until she walked through her front door before he started back. Fortunately, there was little traffic, and he made good time. A few minutes later, he felt the car sway and he slowed down. Then the back of the car suddenly swerved and nearly slid off the road. Soapy stopped and got out to take a look.

The front and back tires on his side were all right. But the right rear end of the car slanted down, and Soapy's heart sank. "Oh, no," he moaned, moving around the back of the car. One glance was enough; his premonition was confirmed. The tire was flat.

"Now you're really in a mess," Soapy told himself, opening the trunk and lifting the spare out. "Now where's the jack?" He searched every inch of the dark trunk, but there was no jack. "No jack?" he cried. "Impossible! There has to be a jack."

He searched the back seat and then the front and under the cushions. But there was no jack anywhere, and not even a lug wrench. "Good thing it happened to me," Soapy muttered. "What if it had been Mitzi?"

The thought was small consolation. Soapy remembered that Mitzi lived near campus and would have had help in five minutes. He turned on the emergency flashers and stood out in the middle of the road in the wet snow. Several cars slowed down until they got past him, but then they sped away.

Soapy walked back to the car and looked at the clock. "Eleven-forty-five," he groaned. "I'll have to walk back to town or get to a phone somewhere. I'm ruined. Mitzi will never speak to me again, if she lets me live."

Then he saw a car slowing down, the lights shining their way through the darkness. The car gradually came to a stop. "Having trouble?" a hearty voice called.

Soapy was almost in tears. "I sure am! I've got a flat, and I don't have a jack or a lug wrench. Or any sense!" he concluded.

"Got a spare?"

"That's all."

"That's enough. Don't worry. We'll have you on your way in five minutes. Come on, guys. Give me a hand."

The speaker, who was about Soapy's age, and two other guys piled out of the car. They grabbed the jack and the lug wrench from their car and went to work. Laughing, talking, and joking, the three worked together as efficiently as a NASCAR pit crew.

ON EMPTY AGAIN!

"There you are," the tallest guy said, straightening up and wiping his hands on his pants. "Take it easy now. Keep it between the lines."

Before Soapy could do any more than mumble his thanks they were back in their car and gone. They left so quickly Soapy never even got their names. The redhead drove more carefully now, and it was 12:15 when he reached Main and Tenth. Grayson's was dark, but the lights from Pete's Place were blazing out through the snow.

"An hour late," Soapy groaned.

He parked in front of the restaurant and peered through the window. Right in his line of vision, sitting at a table facing the door, was the love of Soapy's life.

CHAPTER 6

Night Rider

MITZI SAVRILL, Fireball, Whitty, and Jimmy Chung were sitting together at the first table by the door. Pete, standing behind the counter, saw Soapy first. "Well, look who's here," he said. "The night rider!"

"I'll bet he had car trouble," Fireball said.

"Uh-uh," Whitty corrected. "He had a flat tire."

Mitzi got slowly to her feet. "He could have run out of gas," she said lightly. "There wasn't much in the tank."

"Blonde or brunette, Soapy?" Fireball asked.

Soapy's face turned fiery red. "You know me better than that, Fireball." He turned to Mitzi. "Honest, Mitzi, I had a flat. And there wasn't a jack in the car and, well, I'm sorry I'm late. I guess your parents will be upset, but—"

Mitzi flashed him one of her heartbreaking smiles, and Soapy nearly collapsed. "It's all right, Soapy," she said. "I called home. There's no harm done. Come on. I'll give you all a lift."

NIGHT RIDER

Chip was still awake when he heard Soapy opening the door. He snapped on his desk lamp. The sight that met his eyes gave him a shock. "What happened to you?" he asked, staring at his snow-soaked buddy.

"Oh, man!" Soapy moaned. "Did *I* ever have trouble! What a night."

"What happened? Where were you?"

Soapy briefed Chip on his night's adventure, skipping over certain nonessentials but telling enough about his experience to arouse his friend's sympathy.

"Better take a hot shower and put another blanket on your bed," Chip offered. "Now forget all about it and get some sleep."

Chip's leg was stiff and sore the next morning, but by the end of his last morning class, it had loosened up. He walked briskly across the campus to the student union and found Fireball and Whitty already sitting at the corner table talking to Biggie. They were waiting impatiently for Soapy. "Now what are you guys you up to?" Chip asked.

"You'll see," Fireball said cryptically. "Did you see Soapy when he got home last night?"

Chip smiled. "I sure did."

"Wait!" Whitty cautioned. "Here he comes."

Soapy approached warily. Placing his loaded tray on the table, he edged self-consciously into a chair. "What are you guys so serious about?" he asked.

"We're broke," Whitty said. "How about lending us ten or twenty?"

"Me?" Soapy asked incredulously. "When did I *ever* have any money?"

"Thought you might be carrying a roll," Whitty said, spreading a copy of the *Herald* on the table. "Look at this," he said, tapping the headline. "Right on the front page. Read it!"

At the top of the paper in bold print was the news item:

TRIANGLE MINI MART ROBBED, LONE HOLDUP BANDIT MAKES CLEAN GETAWAY

The fourth in a series of robberies occurred at 11:45 last night at the Triangle Mini Mart. The lone perpetrator obtained more than a hundred dollars. The employee on duty, George Welsh, age sixty-five, described the suspect as young, weighing around 180 pounds, and about six feet in height.

Welsh gave police a good description of the man but was unable to furnish the license number of the car because of the heavy snow. The thief was driving a dark, four-door car with a white top. Welsh was sure the man had purchased gas at the station less than an hour earlier. The police have one important clue to go on.

"Well—" Soapy said, looking from Fireball to Whitty.

"Flat tire?" Whitty commented suggestively. "Black car with a white top," Fireball said thoughtfully. "Hmmm."

Chip and Biggie didn't like it. "Now wait a minute, guys," they said in unison.

"This isn't funny," Biggie added.

Fireball burst out laughing and pointed to Soapy's face. "We're just kidding."

Soapy grinned and shrugged his shoulders nonchalantly. "Sure," he said, "it was easy."

"What did you do with the money?" Fireball asked. "Put it in the flat tire?"

"The police will check *that*," Whitty said, nodding his head wisely.

"Maybe I ought to turn myself in," Soapy suggested.

"Don't worry," Fireball said. "The paper says the bandit made a *clean* getaway. We can give you a perfect alibi. You were as dirty as a coal miner just coming home from work."

Chip glanced at the clock and hastily piled his dishes back on the tray. "Don't you guys have any afternoon classes?" he interrupted. "I've got to hurry. See you tonight."

Dr. Terring showed up before practice that afternoon to check Chip's leg. "Pretty stiff?" he asked.

Chip nodded. "A little. But I think it's better."

"Appears about the same to me," Dr. Terring said. "Are you sure the wish isn't father to the thought?"

"No, sir. It isn't hurting me a bit this afternoon."

Dr. Terring shook his head. "Pain or no pain, the ligament is still swollen. Injuries take time."

"But you said it would be all right if I rested between games."

"I said it *might* be all right." Dr. Terring turned to the trainer. "Excuse him today, Murph. Let him shoot around a little tomorrow, and you watch him."

Chip dressed quickly and caught the downtown bus. When he arrived at Grayson's, Whitty and Fireball were still razzing Soapy.

"Flat tire, huh?"

"Now it says on the front page of the paper . . ."

"I still say it was a blonde."

Chip was caught in the crossfire and watched everything, noting Soapy's quick glance toward Jennifer Andrews and her return wink. Jennifer was also a student at State, and her hours were the same as Soapy's. She finished work at 10:30 each night, while Mitzi seldom completed balancing the slips and cash register before 11:00.

That's the answer, Chip told himself. *Soapy took Jennifer home and had a flat tire, and he doesn't want Mitzi to find it out.*

Murph Kelly let Chip dress Friday afternoon. "Shoot around at the practice basket, Chip, but take it easy."

Coach Corrigan was working the team on the main court. Toward the end of practice, Murph Kelly wandered down to Chip. "How's it going?"

"Not too bad, Murph. If I didn't have to wear the brace, I guess I could move a lot better."

Kelly grinned. "Sure! Sure you could. But the purpose of the brace is to keep the ligament under control. The brace prevents stretching and sudden strains. By the way, Coach has a visitor." He hooked a thumb toward the bleachers.

Coach Corrigan was standing on the sideline, talking to a tall, stoop-shouldered man dressed in sports clothes. "Locke," Kelly said contemptuously. "He's got a lot of nerve busting in here. Coach ought to throw him out."

"Sports need publicity," Chip said significantly, smiling at the angry trainer.

"Not the kind *he* writes. Oh, oh, here he comes. See you later."

Chip had met Jim Locke a number of times and had always felt uncomfortable around him. He thought of the article the caustic writer had written referring to him as Bill Bell's "yes man," and he felt almost antagonistic. Locke's personal appearance was enough to cause an instant dislike by anyone, but Chip had tried to keep his feelings neutral. Now he appraised the man more critically.

The sportswriter had a long, thin nose and a short

mustache and bushy sideburns. His clothes would have been more in keeping with a high-school sophomore. As he approached, Chip moved toward the free-throw line, trying to avoid conversation. But Locke followed him right out on the court.

"Hello, Hilton. What's this? A sort of individual practice?"

"I guess you could call it that, Mr. Locke," Chip calmly replied. "Murph Kelly won't let me do much running."

"Is your leg really that bad?"

"Dr. Terring and Murph seem to think so."

"Well, anyway," Locke said slyly as he sauntered away, "it gives you a chance to practice your shots for Bell's shooting tournament."

Chip was seething inside, but he controlled the impulse to strike back at the sarcastic writer. With a man of Locke's type, it was wiser to ignore anything he said or wrote. Chip got a little consolation from the thought that most of the man's readers were familiar with his exaggerations.

At nine o'clock that evening Mary Hilton called Chip from Valley Falls. She was still worried about his leg and just wanted to talk with him. E-mails were great, but there were times she just wanted to hear his voice— which told her more than words from letters. She and Chip discussed her recent check-up, which had been all clear. Chip and his mom had gone through a difficult challenge a year earlier when she had been diagnosed with cancer. But she was feeling well now, and her surgeon assured her she was fine. "I just have to go in for a check-up every six months, Chip."

Then she skillfully turned the conversation to Chip's knee. She wondered if he should be playing basketball. "Are you giving your knee plenty of rest?"

Chip reassured his mom and told her he was feeling fine. But he wasn't so sure. His leg was throbbing with pain, brace or no brace.

But Saturday morning, when the Statesmen boarded the bus for the Northern State game, Chip was with the team. The other players were relieved when he showed up, and they voiced their feelings.

"You're our good-luck charm, Chipper."

"He sure is—whether he plays or not!"

"I'll play," Chip said stoutly.

Kelly bandaged his knee unusually tight that night. Chip could scarcely move. But he got a break. Northern State used a 2-1-2 zone, and Chip had a picnic. Coach Corrigan set up a 1-3-1 attack. Chip scored twenty-eight points from the field, twelve of them from three-point range, and four free throws for a total of thirty-two points.

But it was still a bitter struggle. Northern played aggressive defense and hustled all the way, and State couldn't work the ball around for the open shots. Chip's three-pointers were the decisive factor, and State eked out a close victory, 77-75.

It was a long bus ride back, and it was made longer because Murph Kelly made the driver stop at frequent intervals. Each time, when the other players got off for something to eat or drink, Kelly kept Chip on the bus and made him walk up and down the aisle.

"I'm moving more now than I did in the game," Chip protested.

"That's what you get for playing," Kelly growled.

The bus reached University at two o'clock in the morning, and Coach Corrigan asked the driver to drop the players off at their dormitories instead of Assembly Hall. Soapy was already asleep. Chip managed to get into bed without waking him up. It seemed as if only a few minutes had passed when he woke up and glanced at the clock. It was nine o'clock, and Soapy's bed was already made. "He's gone downstairs for the papers or out for something for me to eat," Chip murmured.

While Chip waited, half-awake and half-asleep, he thought about Soapy's generous nature and his constant efforts to help his friends. Chip knew a person usually had only a few tried-and-true friends during his whole life, but he was one of the luckiest guys in the world. He had so many friends he could scarcely count them!

Soapy was number one, of course. After the redhead there were so many others—Henry Rockwell, Mr. Grayson, Speed Morris, Biggie Cohen, Red Schwartz, Joel Ohlsen, Jimmy Chung, Fireball Finley, Whitty Whittemore, and Pete Thorpe. And back in Valley Falls there were Doc Jones, Mr. Schroeder, Petey Jackson, and . . .

The next time Chip awakened, Soapy was leaning back in his chair, his size 11 feet propped up on his desk. Amused, Chip watched his pal through half-closed eyes. Soapy was muttering angrily and gritting his teeth.

Chip couldn't restrain himself any longer. "What's so serious?"

Soapy leaped to his feet, his chair tumbling over. "Hey!" he shouted. "You scared me to death! Some game! Nice going! We caught most of it at work." Soapy jabbed the paper. "You see this? Jim Locke again." Soapy shook the paper angrily and read aloud. "'Has Chip Hilton been trying to prove State can't win without him? If so, he is so right!'"

Soapy balled the paper in his hands and hurled it at the wastepaper basket. "How about that guy, Chip?"

Chip cracked his right fist into the palm of his left hand. "I wish—"

"Wish what?"

"Nothing, Soapy. We should know what to expect from Locke by this time. What does Bill Bell say?"

Soapy pointed to the chocolate milk and doughnuts on Chip's desk and sat down again. Picking up the *Herald,* he read silently and then muttered, "That's better."

"What's better?"

"Bell. He says State deserves a lot of credit for its fight. And he says you could help the team even if you had to shoot from the bench. He gives the marksmanship tournament a good plug too. And he says Tech is one of the best teams in the country. They won again last night. That's ten in a row."

Soapy glanced down at his watch. "Oh, I gotta go. See you later. Gotta go on an errand for Mitzi."

"What kind of errand?"

Soapy hesitated. "It's kinda personal, but, well, I'm gonna wash her car. Gotta pay her back for . . . Well, see you later."

"Wait a minute. I'll help you."

"No way! It's my responsibility. And, well—"

Chip grinned and nodded. "I understand. By the way, I want you to know, Soapy, that *I* know exactly why you borrowed Mitzi's car. And I know why you suddenly have an errand that needs doing when it's necessary for me to do a little walking."

Soapy's face fell, and Chip continued quickly. "It's great of you to do it, Soapy. I guess I don't have to tell you what it means to me. Anyway, I guess we understand each other. We always did."

Soapy took off, and Chip got up and dressed slowly. Sipping the milk, he read the front page of the *Herald* and then started for church. After lunch, he hit the books. When Soapy returned a little later, the redhead joined him in study. After dinner, they took a short walk and then hit the books again.

On Monday morning, Chip's knee felt as strong as ever. It seemed even stronger that afternoon when he reported to Murph Kelly. But he couldn't convince the trainer that he should practice. The sports veteran knew all about overconfident athletes.

"Take it easy," Kelly said. "You're not practicing. And tomorrow, you're going to do nothing but shoot a few baskets. Now beat it! And if you're going down to Grayson's, take a cab."

Chip laughed. "You don't care what I do with my money, do you?"

"I care what you do with your money, all right," Kelly growled, "but I want to protect that knee too." He paused briefly and then continued gruffly. "Go on. Get out of here! I'm wasting my breath."

Isaiah Redding arrived from school shortly after Chip reached Grayson's, and they worked steadily until Soapy came in at six o'clock. The redhead rushed into the stockroom and began searching the pockets of his coat. "It's gone!" he said, looking at Chip. "I can't find my receipt for the pictures I'm having developed. I must have dropped it somewhere. I thought it was in the pocket of my jeans. It's just a little stub with some numbers on it. You seen it?"

"No, Soapy. But as long as you have your name on the envelope, they'll give you the photos. Which shop did you use?"

"The one just up the street."

"Wait. I'll go with you."

The photo shop was small. A high counter displaying film and cameras faced the door, and behind it, rows of shelves extended along the wall, all filled with envelopes of developed photographs. Only one employee was behind the counter. "Good evening," she said. "Can I help you?"

"I hope so!" Soapy said. "I'm here to pick up some pictures."

"Do you have your ticket?"

"That's a bit of a problem," Soapy explained. "I lost it."

The young woman smiled. "Well, the ticket is faster, but I'm sure we can find your photos without it. Do you remember the number by any chance?"

"No, I don't."

"Well, let's see if it's entered by your name in the computer." Soapy gave the girl his name, and she punched the keys of her computer. "No, it's not been put in. What was it?"

Soapy explained that it was a roll of thirty-six color prints and also that he'd brought in a negative to have a photograph enlarged.

While he was talking, another customer entered and waited patiently. Soapy stepped aside and addressed the man. "Go ahead, sir. I've lost my receipt, and this may take more time."

"I have plenty of time," the man replied quietly. Meanwhile, the clerk was checking through the bundles, studying the slips on each. She stopped suddenly and pulled a package from a top shelf. "Here we go! Soapy Smith, right?"

"Excuse me," the stranger said, moving up beside Soapy. "Did you say you lost your receipt?"

Soapy turned in surprise. "Yes, sir, I did."

"That's a coincidence," the man said. "I found one. Let's see if they match." He laid a ticket beside the envelope the clerk had placed on the counter. "How about that! Look at the number on the envelope and on this little ticket I have. They're the same: 3646102."

"Yes, they're the same," the clerk agreed.

"Well, I knew I had lost it someplace," Soapy said. "Where did you find it?"

"Perhaps I ought to ask the questions," the man stated quietly. He pulled a small leather case out of his pocket and held it up in front of Soapy's eyes. "I'm Detective Gil Minton, University police. I'd like to ask you a few questions. Down at the station."

CHAPTER 7

The Palm of His Hand

DETECTIVE GIL MINTON drove his black, two-door car swiftly and surely through the evening traffic. He parked in the space marked Detectives Only behind the police station. Then he led the way through a rear door and up several flights of stairs to a small room with two tables, several straight-backed chairs, and a wall phone.

"Have a seat," he said, moving to use the phone. "This is Minton. Ask Fred to come up to room 6, will you, Jim?"

Seconds later, a short, fat man with gray hair entered the room. "What's up, Gil?"

"The photo receipt. This young man is Robert Smith. His ticket checks with the lead I've been following."

The newcomer glanced curiously at Soapy. "I see." Then he glanced at Chip. "And this one?"

"He's a friend of Smith's. Chip Hilton, the State basketball star. This is Detective Fred Parks."

Chip and Soapy nodded, and Detective Minton

continued. "Hilton and Smith both go to school here, and they both work at Grayson's."

Detective Parks sat down behind the table. "How about Hilton? Do we need him?"

"Not necessarily, Fred. He wanted to come."

"All right, it's not important." He turned to Soapy. "*Now,* Smith, we have to ask you some questions. Detective Minton is going to write down the answers, so think carefully before you answer."

"But what's this all about?" Soapy asked indignantly. "I'm no criminal. I've never been in trouble in my life."

"That's right," Chip added. "We grew up together. I think we ought to be told what you're trying to find out. You don't have to worry about Soapy. He'll tell you everything he knows about anything!"

"Take it easy, Hilton," Detective Minton said gently. "You'll find out all you need to know in a few minutes. Relax, please."

Detective Parks cleared his throat impatiently. "Now, if everyone will be quiet for a few minutes, we can get this over with. Where were you last Wednesday night, Smith?"

Soapy was obviously worried. He glanced at Chip and hesitated briefly before answering. "I was working at the store. At Grayson's."

"Do you have a driver's license?"

"Yes, sir."

"Do you have a car?"

"No, sir."

"Were you in a car last Wednesday night?"

"No, sir. Oh, wait! That was the night of the Cathedral game. Yes, sir, I was. I borrowed Mitzi Savrill's car to drive Chip home from the game. He has a bad leg."

"I know. Who is Mitzi Savrill?"

"She's the cashier and bookkeeper at Grayson's."

"What color is Mitzi Savrill's car?"

Soapy considered a second. "It's blue with a white top."

The detectives exchanged significant glances. Then Parks continued his interrogation. "What time did you borrow the car?"

"About 10:15."

"You drove Hilton home. Then what did you do?"

Soapy hesitated. "Well, I got gas, then I started back to Grayson's—"

"And?"

"And I had a flat tire."

"Where?"

"About three or four miles from Grayson's."

Parks nodded thoughtfully. "What were you doing way out there?"

"I—I was just taking a ride."

"What time was it then?"

Soapy deliberated. "It was about 11:40."

"You were alone in the car?"

"Yes, sir. That is—yes, sir."

"What time did you return the car to Miss Savrill?"

"It was about 12:15, sir."

"Now, Smith, did you stop anywhere during those two hours?"

Soapy hesitated again. "No, sir. That is, only when I had the flat tire."

"Did you talk to anyone?"

"Yes, sir. To the guys who changed the tire."

Detective Parks questioned Soapy in detail about the exact time they arrived to help him change the tire, who they were, the time they left, and how fast he drove the car back to the restaurant. During the questioning, Detective Minton kept scribbling in his writing pad.

THE PALM OF HIS HAND

Chip wanted to call Grayson's to let them know what had happened, but he also didn't want to leave Soapy. He was relieved when Detective Parks suggested they take a little drive. Soapy and Detective Parks got in the back seat, and Chip sat in the front with Minton, who was driving. Chip was determined to stick with Soapy and find out what it was all about. He wasn't kept long in doubt.

Detective Minton drove rapidly up Main Street and out toward State's campus. Just before the main drive, he turned into the Triangle Mini Mart. "This is as far as we go," he said, turning off the ignition.

Chip recognized the station, and a realization seized him. *The robbery! So that's what this is all about!*

Inside the store, Detective Parks got right to the point. He waved a hand toward Chip and Soapy. "Recognize either of these two, Welsh? Can you identify either one of them?"

"This is ridiculous," Chip said hotly.

"Hold it, Hilton!" Parks said sharply. He turned to the man behind the counter. "Well, Welsh?"

Welsh took off his glasses and wiped them with his handkerchief. Ignoring Chip, he stepped from behind the counter and pranced around Soapy like a bantam rooster, looking at the redhead from one side and then the other. He stopped and shook his head uncertainly. Then he put on his glasses and walked around Soapy again.

"Hmmm," he said. "About the same size, all right. Red hair too! And a fat nose. He looks like him, but I can't be sure. I told you the guy had one of those plastic see-through masks on. Now if he had on a hat—"

"A hat!" Soapy exploded. "I never wore a hat in my life. A baseball cap, yes, but a hat, that's for old peop—"

Then Soapy blushed as he saw Detective Parks holding his hat at his side. "Er, I've only been in this gas station twice in my life. Once with Chip and once last week during the storm."

"That's enough, Smith," Parks said, shaking Soapy's arm. "You be quiet. Well, Welsh?"

The grouchy man shook his head uncertainly. "The guy was wearing a hat," he said sullenly. "An old brown hat with—"

"Here!" Detective Parks interrupted, placing his own hat on Soapy's head. "How's that?"

"Well," Welsh drawled reluctantly, "it's not brown, and I can't be sure. Now if he only had on an old blue sweater—"

Parks grabbed the hat off Soapy's head and jammed it back on his own head. "Look, Welsh, we can't carry a whole wardrobe around. Is this the kid or not?"

"Well," Welsh drawled, "as I said, I didn't get a very good look at his face, especially with that mask. But if you put him in the car over by the last pump and have him walk into the store, I might get the whole picture better in my mind."

"All right," Parks said patiently. "We'll try that!" Parks and Soapy walked out to the car while Gil Minton and Welsh stayed inside. Chip seized the opportunity to call Grayson's.

Mitzi answered the phone, and Chip explained what had happened. "This doesn't seem right. Tell Mr. Grayson, Mitzi. And hurry! Mitzi, please don't say anything about it to anyone else."

By the time Chip finished the call, Soapy was sitting in the car behind the wheel. He got out and walked into the store.

"Well," Minton said, turning to Welsh, "now what?"

"Well, it was snowing," Welsh said uncertainly, "and my glasses were all wet. I'd just been outside throwing trash in the dumpster."

Detective Minton turned away, shrugging his shoulders. "Now he wants snow!"

"*Listen,* Welsh," Detective Parks said more roughly than he intended, "we can't stay here all night. Now I know it was 11:45 at night, and it was dark, and your glasses were all clouded up, and the man wore a brown hat, a mask you could partially see through, and a blue sweater, and you thought he had red hair.

"And when he finished pumping the gas, he came inside, just after you'd come in from emptying the trash. He poked a gun in your back and asked for the money in the register. And then he made you lie down on the floor and said he would shoot if you came outside before he drove away."

Detective Parks was almost shouting now. He paused for breath and then said, "Now for the last time, is this the man?"

Before Welsh could answer, there was an interruption. A car screeched to a stop directly in front of the door. George Grayson leaped out of the car and hurried toward the group. "What's going on, Chip?" he asked.

"Just a minute—" Parks began roughly. Then he recognized Grayson. "Oh! Mr. Grayson. I—"

"Hello, Parks, Minton. What's going on here?"

"Give us a second, Mr. Grayson. We'll explain everything." Parks turned back to Welsh. "All right. Is this the man or not?"

"As I was saying," Welsh persisted, "all these young kids look alike nowadays and—"

"All right, all right, Welsh," Parks said in resignation. "That's enough."

HARDCOURT UPSET

"Now can I have an explanation?" George Grayson asked.

Parks's attitude was conciliatory but firm. "We're just doing our duty, Mr. Grayson. Undoubtedly you know that we've had a number of convenience store robberies during the last two months. This place was robbed last Wednesday, and Robert Smith's photo receipt was found here near the counter the same night. So we've been asking him a few questions."

"I told you I stopped here for gas that night," Soapy said. "But I didn't rob anyone. That night or any other night."

"Is everything cleared up now?" Grayson asked.

Parks shook his head. "Not quite, sir. You see, Smith admits he was using a car that night that matches the description of the car Welsh says the robber was driving. Further, his explanation of his travels that night is vague and unsatisfactory. Besides, there is a discrepancy in time to be accounted for.

"He told us that he had a flat tire three or four miles out on West Main Street, which is cause for considerable conjecture since he can't give us a good reason for being in that vicinity. The flat tire could have happened anywhere. A block from here or several miles away. So far, he hasn't accounted for his whereabouts at 11:45, the exact time of the robbery."

"I can see your position, Parks," Grayson said understandingly, "but from what I've heard, this man's identification is worthless. And I'm not too sure I like your procedures here either."

"Now you listen here," Welsh began. "I—"

Detective Minton stopped Welsh. "We have to start *somewhere*, Mr. Grayson," he said slowly. "If Smith now would only be a little more specific—"

THE PALM OF HIS HAND

"But you can't keep the boy out here all night just because you found a ticket. He admits stopping here for gas, and he's certainly explained the car satisfactorily."

"That's right, Mr. Grayson, but the other details aren't very clear."

"They can surely wait. I know he will be able to explain everything to your satisfaction when he's had a chance to collect his wits. I'll vouch for him. Suppose we get together tomorrow afternoon in my office. I think we can clear this thing up quickly enough as far as Soapy is concerned."

"All right, Mr. Grayson," Parks said decisively. "That's all right with us."

"I'll vouch for him. I know you men both realize it's extremely important to Soapy that all of this be kept confidential. It's important to me too."

"Don't worry about our end," Minton said. "We never give out information on routine investigations. I don't suppose Smith or Hilton are going to do much talking about it."

"You can be sure of that," Grayson said grimly.

Parks turned to Soapy with a brief smile. "Don't leave town, young man."

"Leave town!" Soapy gasped. "Why would I leave town? I like it here. I'm stayin' here until I graduate from State."

The two detectives drove away, and George Grayson headed for the phone. Chip and Soapy listened to Welsh's garrulous chatter while they waited.

"Detectives!" Welsh snorted. "Hah! They couldn't catch a cold." He peered suspiciously at Soapy. "If they had only put a *brown* hat on your head and got me a blue sweater, I'd have known for sure. You got a brown hat? Bet you do!"

"I never had a hat in my life," Soapy said. "Unless you call a sailor cap a hat. I had my picture taken in one of those when I was two years old."

Welsh grunted sarcastically. "Bein' smart, eh? Won't do you any good to get smart with me. I got you right here." He tapped the palm of his hand. "All I need is a brown hat with a coupla fishin' feathers stuck in the hat-band. Green ones!"

"But you haven't identified him," Chip said shortly.

Welsh looked Chip up and down, the expression on his face clearly contemptuous. "Well, now, maybe I have and maybe I haven't, bub."

"I don't see how you could identify a person with a mask on, as you claim, even if he *did* put on a sweater and a brown hat," Chip countered,

"There's nothing wrong with my eyes, college smart aleck," Welsh blustered.

George Grayson returned then, and the conversation ended. On the way back to Grayson's, Chip and Soapy filled in the missing parts of the night's adventure. Their employer listened intently, stopping them from time to time to clear up certain details. "We'll straighten it out tomorrow afternoon," Grayson said confidently. "Now you had better get back on the job. On second thought, I better go in first. We don't want to attract too much attention. Suppose you stop for a few minutes at Pete's Place." He patted Soapy's shoulder. "Now don't worry. Everything is going to be all right."

The two boys found an empty booth in the little restaurant and talked it over while they drank their Cokes. "That's some man," Soapy said in admiration. "Did he ever take charge!"

"Yes, but I'm worried, Soapy," Chip said. "What *were* you doing all that time?"

"I told you I had a flat."

"But what were you doing all the way out on Main Street? You had to go right past the store. Where were you going?"

"Man, Chip, what's that got to do with it?"

"Everything. You're under suspicion." Chip let that sink in and then said, "I know you wouldn't do anything wrong, Soapy. I've got a hunch you took Jennifer home. Right?"

Soapy nodded. "Yes, that's right, Chip."

"Well, why didn't you say so? What's wrong with taking her home? Mitzi would understand that."

"Sure. Sure, I guess so, Chip. I just didn't want to get Jennifer involved with Parks and Minton."

They sat without speaking for a long minute, each thinking of the night's events—and its implications. Chip broke the silence. "The police don't know you from Adam. And what's more important, you can't expect them to believe *anything* if you don't tell them *everything*. That's logical enough, isn't it?"

"Sure, Chip."

"Do you remember what my mom always said about telling the truth?"

"Sure I do," Soapy said. "'Always tell the truth, and then you never have to remember what you said.'"

CHAPTER 8

California, Here We Come!

LATER THAT NIGHT, after they had gone back to their dorm room, Chip began to question Soapy again. "Soapy," he said gently, "try to get the time element straightened out in your mind. The detectives seem to feel it's important."

"I know, Chip. I *am* trying."

"What time did you get Jennifer home?"

"It was exactly 11:25. Jen checked the time on her watch."

"Did you start right back?"

"Sure. But I didn't get far. That's when I had the flat tire. About five minutes after I dropped her off. And it was about ten minutes before those three guys came along."

"What time was it then?"

"About 11:40. And it was 11:55 when they left. I checked that when I got in the car. And it was exactly 12:15 when I reached the restaurant. The roads were icy, and I was being very careful with Mitzi's car."

CALIFORNIA, HERE WE COME!

"That's better," Chip said. "Now stick to that."

There was no sound in the room for a few minutes, but just as Chip was dozing off, Soapy spoke once more. "Chip, *you* don't think Mitzi will be angry because I took Jennifer home, do you?"

"I think she would be extremely angry if you hadn't. Me too! I *do* think you could have stopped at the store and told her where you were going though. Now let's get some sleep."

Neither of them got much sleep that night. Chip heard his roommate tossing and turning, and in the morning they were both dead tired. Soapy was concerned about Chip's knee but avoided further reference to the robbery.

Chip skipped the usual lunch meeting with his pals and instead went to see Mr. Grayson to tell him what he had learned from Soapy. George Grayson was pleased. "I'm glad to hear about Jennifer," he said. "Why didn't he just tell Minton that? Oh, well, that's Soapy. But it clears up a lot of things. You leave everything to me."

When Chip reported for practice, Murph Kelly sent him out on the floor to warm up his knee by shooting baskets. Chip didn't benefit much from that practice. Accurate shooting requires absolute concentration, and Chip was in no mood to concentrate on anything except Soapy's predicament.

A little later, the trainer came up to watch practice and noticed Chip's inaccurate marksmanship. He sauntered down to the practice basket to find out the trouble. "What's the matter, Chip? Is your knee bothering you?"

"No, Murph, something else. Do you mind if I call it a day?"

"Mind? What do you think? This has got to be a first. Beat it!"

Chip dressed quickly and caught a ride with a classmate who was heading downtown. Chip hopped out of the car at the corner and hustled up to the front entrance of the store. Then he walked casually through the door and up to the cashier's desk. On the way, he glanced at the fountain. Soapy was nowhere in sight.

"Hello, Chip," Mitzi said gently. "Mr. Grayson wants to see you. He's in his office."

"Where's Soapy?"

"Mr. Grayson sent him around to Pete's Place to eat. He had a pretty long afternoon."

"Are the cops gone?"

Mitzi nodded. "Just a few minutes ago. They looked at the car and asked me about letting Soapy use it. I guess they're satisfied."

"I'm sure glad to hear that. Thanks, Mitzi."

Ann Tracy was typing busily when Chip went upstairs to the main offices. She smiled and nodded her head toward the inner office. "Go right in, Chip. Mr. Grayson is expecting you."

George Grayson looked up and nodded toward a vacant chair. "Well, so far, so good. I told Parks and Minton about Jennifer, and they talked to her, and she verified that part of Soapy's story."

Chip breathed a sigh of relief. "Then everything is all right—"

"Not quite. Parks and Minton claim Soapy could have taken her home and still have gotten back to the mini mart by 11:45. Soapy isn't going to be in the clear until they locate the men who helped him with the tire and verify the time. By the way, I sent Soapy down to Pete's Place. Why don't you drop in down there and talk to him?"

Soapy was sitting in a rear booth at the restaurant, eating a sandwich when Chip slid into the opposite seat.

He looked up in surprise. "Chip! What's wrong? Didn't you go to practice?"

"Sure I went to practice."

"Is your knee worse?"

"No, it's all right." Chip waved his hand in dismissal. "I want to hear about you. What happened?"

"Well, they asked a lot of questions and talked to Mitzi and Jennifer, and then they looked at the car. But they don't seem to be satisfied about the flat tire."

"How do you know?"

"Chip, I could just tell by the questions they asked. Parks would say: 'Now, Smith, put yourself in my place. Wouldn't you think it strange if I told you that three guys came along in a car and helped me out of a lot of trouble, and I didn't even ask their names or remember what they looked like or where they lived or notice the kind of car they were driving?'

"And I said, 'Yes, sir, Mr. Parks, I would.'

"Then Minton would say: 'I don't understand how you can be so sure about the *exact* time you picked up Jennifer Andrews and the *exact* time you had the flat tire and the *exact* time they got the spare on the car and the *exact* time you reached Grayson's. It's just too *exact*.'"

"What did you say to that?"

"I told him it was all a coincidental—"

"Coincidence."

"Well, a series of coincidents. Just like the stuff about the photo receipt and the car and the time was circumstantial."

"Then what?"

"Well, they both laughed and Minton said something about a lot of double talk. Then they got serious again and said they were going to concentrate on finding the three guys."

"Was that all?"

Soapy frowned sadly. "All? Sure! That's all—all I heard for three hours."

"Three hours!" Chip echoed. "No wonder you're down. Well, come on, we'll be through work in three hours. Then we're going straight home to sit down and figure out how to locate those three guys who helped you with the tire."

"Chip, is it OK if we don't use Mitzi's car for awhile? We can take the bus back to the dorm."

Chip smiled and nodded. "You got it, bud."

Immediately after work, Chip and Soapy caught a bus to the campus. They were in their room at 10:45. Chip went right to work.

"Now why *didn't* you get the names of those guys?"

"Chip, it was snowing a wet snow. And we were all soaking wet. No one wanted to talk."

"Couldn't you see their faces?"

"Sure, but I didn't pay any attention."

"Which one did the most talking?"

"Well, the tall guy, I guess."

"How tall? How heavy?"

"Come on, Chip, how do I know? You're worse than Parks and Minton!"

"Soapy, just close your eyes and think. Try to visualize the guy," Chip suggested.

As Soapy closed his eyes and wrinkled up his nose, Chip prompted. "Was he as tall as Sky?"

Soapy's eyes flashed open, and he pointed at Chip. "No, he was more like you, Chip. He was about six-three or four, I guess. About 190 pounds."

"Good. That's a start, but you must have noticed something else. A ring or a watch or glasses, or—"

Soapy leaped to his feet. "Yes! That's it! He was

wearin' glasses. They were cloudy, and he kept saying he couldn't see without them and he couldn't see with them."

"What kind of clothes was he wearing?"

Soapy sighed. "Chip, I told you it was snowing and then raining. How could I tell what he had on? Besides, he was wearing a raincoat."

"What kind of raincoat?"

"It was one of those plastic-looking things."

"Now, how about his features?"

"He had a long nose," Soapy said wearily, dropping back on his pillow.

"What kind of lips? Thin or full?"

Soapy sat up suddenly and jerked open his desk drawer. "Hey! I've got an idea. You're good at drawing, right? Why don't you draw a picture of the guy?" He tossed a notebook to Chip and stretched out on the bed once more. "OK. Now let's have the questions."

"I'm not that good," Chip protested.

"Well, you'll do better than my stick figures. Try it."

Chip began to sketch the outline of a face, carefully drawing in the nose and the mouth. "What about his eyes? Do you remember the color?"

"You kidding? In that weather? Behind those glasses? All I know is he had eyes."

"How about the eyebrows and eyelashes?"

"He had kinda bushy eyebrows. Yeah, and he had black hair. His hood slipped back accidentally once."

"Short hair?"

"No. Well, it wasn't short and it wasn't long. But it was kinda wavy and bushy—like his eyebrows. That's why I noticed it."

Chip grunted. "Good. Now we're getting somewhere."

Soapy got up and looked over Chip's shoulder. "Hey! That's perfect. That's him!"

Chip laughed. "It can't be that good."

"But it is! What are you going to do with it?"

"I don't know exactly. But at least I know about what he looks like."

"Man!" Soapy exclaimed, picking up the paper. "It's just like one of those cartoons in the paper."

Chip banged the desk with his fist. "That's it! The papers! We'll run an ad in the University papers and the campus paper too."

"An ad? What for?"

"For the three guys."

Soapy nodded thoughtfully. Then his face lit up like a neon light. "You've got it!" he said enthusiastically. "We'll offer a reward."

"All right, how does this sound? Listen: 'Important! Three men who helped change a tire last Wednesday night on West Main Street at approximately 11:45 P.M., please write to box such-and-such in care of this newspaper. Reward.'"

Soapy was exuberant. "Sounds great. This is getting interesting." His face sobered. "But suppose those guys don't see it?"

"Then we'll try something else. I'm going to sleep. Tomorrow's a big day."

"You playing against Mercer tomorrow night?"

"I sure am. I'm going to make the Western trip too. It'll be a relief to get away from all this cold weather."

"You'll have a great time, Chip. Imagine! All the way out to Oregon and then down to California!" Soapy's enthusiasm suddenly disappeared, and his brow furrowed as he turned out the light. "You gonna be able to play two days in a row, Chip?"

"Sure. I'm through babying my knee. Pleasant dreams, Soapy."

CALIFORNIA, HERE WE COME!

Chip didn't do any dreaming that night. He wished he hadn't said anything about the trip. *Way to go,* he rebuked himself bitterly. *You go away on the best trip of the year, and your best friend stays behind up to his freckled ears in trouble. Some loyalty . . .*

Despite his sleepless night, Chip woke up before Soapy on Wednesday morning. And for the second day in a row, Soapy did not rush downstairs to get their copy of the *News.*

On the way to their first class, Soapy mentioned it. "You know, Chip," he said wryly, "Jim Locke's column has suddenly become *extremely* unimportant."

"That's what I've been trying to tell you all along," Chip said quietly. "And that reminds me. I've got to put the ad in the papers. See you this afternoon."

"How about lunch with the crew?"

"I won't have time."

"I guess I'll skip it too," Soapy said thoughtfully. "I've got to hit the books."

Chip carried the picture of Soapy's worried face in his mind's eye all day—in every class and in the advertising offices of the *News,* the *Herald,* and the *Statesman.*

And that night in the game with Mercer, Chip forgot all about his knee. He was tired physically, but he pushed himself savagely and recklessly, cutting and driving and hustling as if he had never heard of a strained ligament. He was awkward and stiff, but he hit for thirty-five points in the thirty minutes he played. State won 83-77.

It was the third win in a row for the Statesmen, and Chip's teammates were riding high again. In the locker room, while Murph was checking out Chip's knee, the guys really cut loose.

"Yeah!" Thornhill yelped, snapping King with his towel. "A little summer weather for a change."

HARDCOURT UPSET

"Three in a row!" Bradley Gowdy cried.

"Thanks to Chip," King said, grabbing the towel out of Thornhill's hands.

"Thirty-five points!" Jimmy Chung yelled excitedly.

"Now we're rolling," Barkley shouted from the shower. "California, here we come!"

Chowder and Sourdough Bread

MITZI SAVRILL, Soapy Smith, Jane Adams, and Jennifer Andrews were all talking at once and laughing as they drove to University's airport early Thursday morning.

It had snowed during the night, and the roads were still icy, but the salt trucks were out. Snow was piled high along the sides of the streets and sidewalks. Once they arrived at the airport, the lot was nearly full. It was a long walk from their parking place to the terminal, and the cold wind whipped around, chilling them until they shivered. They were relieved to get inside and join the warmth of the excited crowd.

And what a crowd! The concourse was jammed! While waiting for the flight, the State University basketball team talked and joked with what seemed hundreds of fans who had come to see the team off in a show of support. Business travelers ducked red-and-blue State pennants as they tried to weave their way through the fans clogging the concourse.

Mitzi and Soapy spied Chip standing with Speed and threaded their way through the crowd to reach them. Mitzi was determined to have a few words alone with Chip. She smiled brightly at Soapy and, pointing to one of the shops, suggested it would be nice to get some magazines for the guys to read.

As soon as Soapy turned away, Mitzi nodded at Speed and grasped Chip by the arm. She led him a few paces away. "Don't worry about Soapy while you're gone, Chip. Mr. Grayson said to tell you he would take care of everything." She smiled up at Chip reassuringly. "And I'll help. Soapy is one of the nicest guys I have ever known."

"He thinks you're pretty wonderful, too. 'Course you would never know that, would ya?" Chip said, smiling into her sincere violet-blue eyes. "Oh, by the way, maybe you can do something about Fireball and Whitty. They're kidding the life out of Soapy about the car. We haven't told them about his trouble with the police. Maybe if you told Cindy, she could get them to lay off."

"I'll take care of that," Mitzi said firmly.

Soapy came rushing back with an armful of *Sports Illustrated* magazines and several bags of Gummi bears. "These ought to hold you guys all the way to Oregon," the redhead said happily, looking from Chip to Mitzi and then back again. "Hey," he continued suspiciously, "what have you two been talking about?"

Chip grinned fondly at his best friend. "Aren't your ears burning?"

Soapy shook his head uncertainly and rubbed first his left and then his right ear. "Uh-uh. Not a bit."

"Well, they ought to be," Chip said, adding hastily, "but it was all good."

CHOWDER AND SOURDOUGH BREAD

The gate crew announced the departure of flight 6 for Chicago and the West. "Passengers please board through gate 4."

"That's us," Speed said, rejoining the trio. "We're on our way."

Chip paused as he started down the corridor. He turned around. Soapy and Mitzi were still standing there, watching him leave. Chip waved another farewell, his heart heavy at leaving Soapy alone with all his trouble.

Chip and Speed had seats together and quickly settled in. It was a smooth flight to Chicago. Chip slept and Speed read Soapy's magazines. They landed in Chicago with scarcely a tremor, and in a few minutes the seats of the deplaning passengers were filled, and the plane took off once again.

A short time later, the flight attendants came through the aisle, serving lunch. Chip was enjoying the flight immensely, although nothing was visible through the window except big, lazy clouds. Listening to the steady hum of the engine, he felt as though it were suspended in the sky.

The plane was warm and cozy, and Chip was dozing when the captain announced the plane would be landing in Denver in a few minutes and that the State basketball team would disembark. "The crew and I wish you good luck," he said heartily. "If we're lucky, we may get to see you play Saturday night in the Cow Palace."

The team liked that and gave the crew a big hand. Then the plane began its swift descent. It broke through the clouds, and down below, the city of Denver came swiftly into view, completely covered with snow. Chip and Speed were looking out their window when the plane eased down onto a runway between two high banks of snow that towered above the wings of the plane.

"Where's that warm weather you were talking about, Andy?" Bill King yelled. "This is worse than University. We'd better get some snowshoes!"

"This is great ski country. I could live here!" Speed exclaimed, putting down the *Denver Post's* sports section.

Fifty minutes later, the Statesmen boarded a smaller jet that carried them to Salem, the capital of Oregon. Some scoffed at the bus that carried them over the snowbound roads to Gilbert, but most of them were glad to be back on firm ground. Coach Corrigan gave them the evening off. Most of the players went to the movies. Chip remained in his room, studying and resting his leg—and thinking about Soapy and his problem.

Friday dawned bright and sunny and warm. Coach Corrigan held a brief strategy session and then arranged for a bus tour of the Gilbert area.

The game that night was fought hard all the way, but State led at the end to win by two, 66-64. Chip was needed in the second half. His thirty-one points were a high for both teams.

Saturday and Sunday were two of the most interesting days of Chip's life. The sky was completely clear on the flight down the coast to San Francisco, and the beautiful shoreline was clearly visible all the way. The drive from the airport to the city led past the Cow Palace. Located ten miles from the center of the city in an industrial section, it seemed a strange setting for a sports arena. It had opened in 1941 to exhibit livestock and now hosted a myriad of events, from rodeos to the circus to World Wide Federation to concerts and antique shows.

Chip forgot all about that when he learned Murph Kelly had instructed the bus driver to give a short tour. He became absorbed in the interesting scenes of the great city: world-renowned Nob Hill; the Powell Street cable cars; Fisherman's Wharf; Market Street; Telegraph Hill; and Grant Avenue, the heart of the city's Chinatown. Jimmy Chung gave detail after detail as the group visited Chinatown. Later, the bus driver went along The Embarcadero toward Fisherman's Wharf. The team piled off the bus and found places to eat as they waited for the ferry to take them to Alcatraz. Speed, Jimmy, Sky, Bitsy, and Chip stopped at the Lobster Pot. Each ate sourdough bread and several bowls of chowder before discovering the delights of Ghirardelli chocolate.

"I could live on this chowder and sourdough bread!" Bitsy exclaimed.

"Only if you added Ghirardelli chocolates too," Speed chimed in.

It was a busy day that ended with a good rest at their hotel before they headed to the Cow Palace for the game.

More than twelve thousand spectators were jammed into the arena by game time. State's opponent, College of the West, was rated as one of the nation's top teams. The Westerners had lost to Templeton in the Holiday Invitational Tournament. Then State and Templeton had battled right down to the wire in the semifinals, but State emerged the winner. Chip had been injured on an attempted shot just as the buzzer ending the game sounded. Then, barely able to stand, he had dropped in a pair of free throws to win the game by the narrow margin of one point, 76-75.

This was the same kind of game. The lead changed hands with almost every score, and the fans were on their feet and cheering the brilliant performance of both teams right down to the last play of the game.

Coach Corrigan used Chip sparingly; he was trying to protect and rest him, yet still win the game. With

HARDCOURT UPSET

College of the West leading 94-92 and twenty seconds left to play, Jimmy Chung dribbled around his opponent and hit with a desperate two-pointer to tie the score.

On the Westerners' inbounding after the State basket, Jimmy pulled the old decoy act, pivoting just in time to deflect the ball. The intended receiver and Jimmy dove for the ball at the same instant. The referee called it a held ball when the mad scramble ended. The possession arrow favored College of the West. It was almost certain the Westerners would play the last shot for the win or certainly for overtime.

Speed Morris became the hero then, taking a desperate chance on the inbound pass. He timed it just right, streaked in front of the Westerners' big center, and intercepted the ball. Barkley immediately called for a time-out.

There were four seconds left to play. The score was tied at 94-94, and every fan in the Cow Palace was standing. In the huddle, Corrigan told the Statesmen to set up their box out-of-bounds formation and to work the block so Chip would get the final shot. The horn sounded, and Barkley took the ball out of bounds.

Chip was in the outside corner position of the box, and when Barkley slapped the ball, he broke out of his position and cut around the pick. Kirk's pass was fast and sure and Chip's fifteen-foot jump shot ripped through the cords just as the final buzzer ended the game. The final score: State 96, College of the West, 94.

Chip's thirty-eight points were high for the night, but they were expensive tallies. He could scarcely walk off the court. Murph Kelly helped him to the locker room, growling angrily on the way. And while the Statesmen celebrated the concluding victory of their Western trip, the veteran trainer worked grimly on Chip's knee.

CHOWDER AND SOURDOUGH BREAD

Everyone thought Sunday was the perfect end to the West Coast trip. Kelly announced that the coaching staff had arranged for Sunday brunch at the Top of the Mark. The elevators shot swiftly upward nineteen floors, and the players were led to tables beside the floor-to-ceiling windows. Below was the breathtaking 360-degree, sky-line view of San Francisco and the bay.

The international port stretched out below them with shipyards, anchored vessels, Alcatraz, famous Treasure Island, which was used as a Far East debarking point for the armed forces in World War II, the famous Golden Gate Bridge, and many other wonderful sights.

As Sky passed by the coaching staff on his third trip through the buffet line, he joked, "Hey, Murph, how about asking the coaches to schedule us some games in Hawaii next year? Or better yet, how about Alaska?"

Chip was enthralled by the splendor, but he didn't forget his best friend. His heart took a sharp dip as he thought how much Soapy would have enjoyed all these wonders. The thought dampened his spirits, and he was glad when the team was on its way to San Francisco International Airport.

On the plane, after closing the overhead bin, Chip sat back, tired and worried. It had been a wonderful trip and great to win two tough games, but he felt he belonged back in University, helping his friend Soapy.

Chip was sleeping soundly when a flight attendant shook his shoulder. "We'll be landing in University in a few minutes," he said. "Put your seatback up, please."

Chip peered down at the snow-covered ground below. University was coming into view. Chip glanced at his watch. It was exactly seven o' clock. When the plane glided to a stop in front of the terminal, the players headed for the doors, their fatigue forgotten. It was good to be back home with two tough games under their belts and five straight wins behind them.

As Chip walked up the corridor, he looked ahead to the crowd waiting to greet the team. And there were Soapy and Mitzi waiting inside the door, just as he had left them. "I might have known." He smiled to himself. "I hope they have good news."

Soapy was beaming when Chip approached, but Mitzi's solemn expression was foreboding. "Nice going, Chipper," the redhead cried. "Your knee all right?"

"I'm OK, Soapy. Hello, Mitzi. Any news?"

"Not yet," Mitzi replied glumly.

"Sure there's news!" Soapy said quickly, pulling a paper out of his pocket. "Look at this! In the *News,* no less." He pointed to the headline and read it aloud: "'Hilton stars on State's victorious road trip.' Great, right?"

"That isn't the kind of news I meant. What about the ad?"

Soapy turned quickly away. "I'll go ahead to the baggage claim with the guys and get your bag for you, Chip. Meet you down there by the bus."

Mitzi grasped Chip's arm as soon as Soapy was out of hearing. "No one has answered the ad so far, Chip."

"They will," Chip said confidently.

"Well, maybe," Mitzi said uncertainly, "but they better hurry."

"Why?"

"Well, the man at the mini mart has changed his mind. He now says Soapy is the robber!"

CHAPTER 10

Word of Honor

GEORGE GRAYSON leaned back in his chair and shook his head. "But it isn't circumstantial evidence, Chip. It's a positive identification."

"But Welsh couldn't identify Soapy that first time. What makes him so sure now?"

"I don't know. Parks and Minton are worried about this new development because it puts them on the spot. However, I checked the dates of several of the earlier robberies. A redheaded man matching Welsh's general description held up the City Service Station the same night the team won the tournament at Springfield."

"Soapy was in Springfield that night," Chip said quickly. "The whole team could testify to that."

George Grayson nodded. "There's no question about that, and it's got them stumped. But Welsh's boss, the owner of the mini mart, is pressing for action, and we've got to act fast. We've got to find those three who helped Soapy that night."

Chip got to his feet. "How much time do we have?"

"That I don't know. But I do know that Parks and Minton have got to move. They're not completely sold on Welsh's identification, but they have to keep after Soapy until he's completely in the clear."

"They've been giving him a bad time, all right," Chip said ruefully.

"Did Soapy tell you that?"

"No, sir. But I know Soapy about as well as I know myself, I guess. Anyway, every time I mention the ad, he changes the subject."

Grayson nodded. "That's Soapy. Chip, we've got one serious problem. If Welsh begins to talk and raise a fuss, we're all going to be on the spot. Parks, Minton, you, me, everyone concerned."

"I can understand that, sir."

"This robbery is probably the only sensational thing Welsh has ever experienced," Grayson said. "He would probably identify *me* as the robber if he thought he could get his picture in the paper."

"There's not much doubt of that, sir."

"And," George Grayson continued thoughtfully, "if some reporter like Jim Locke, if there is another reporter like him, should hear Welsh's story, Soapy's picture would be plastered all over the front page."

That brought the danger right out in the open, and Chip thoughtfully considered the importance of the words. What to do?

George Grayson interrupted Chip's thoughts. "I'm behind Soapy all the way. I'm sure you are aware of that. But we *must* find those three. If there is any way I can help, count on me. I don't want to be trite, but I'm as close as your phone, here at the store or at home."

Chip forgot all about school, basketball, work, and

everything else except Soapy's problem. He spent the rest of the morning in the stockroom trying to think of a new angle. But he arrived at only one important conclusion: he needed help, and he could no longer keep Soapy's secret from the rest of their friends.

Chip found Soapy eating lunch alone in the student union. He told Soapy they needed to tell the rest of the guys about the robbery. Chip was relieved when the redhead agreed. Then Chip went into action.

Pete's Place was practically empty when he stopped in for a burger. With Chip's lunch, Pete brought over a copy of the *Herald*. "Nice shooting, Chip. Bill Bell gives you a big plug here in the paper. Listen: 'Chip Hilton's sensational hoop scoring under fire proves his national marksmanship title is not a stand-around, practice-shot crown.

"'Hilton has scored 421 points in 333 minutes of play to give the reigning champion an average of nearly 1.3 points per minute and slightly over 32 points per game.'

"How's that? And listen to this: 'The National Marksmanship Tournament has caught on all over the country, and Chip Hilton's crown will be the goal of the greatest list of sharpshooters in the history of the event. The local AAU office has been swamped by entries for the State finals to be held here on February 11 and 12.'

"Neat writing, huh? Hey, what's the matter, Chip? You sick?"

"No, I'm all right, Pete. Just worried, that's all."

"You're worried! How about Corrigan and the fans and everyone else around here? We're just as worried about that knee as you are."

"It's not my knee, Pete. It's something a lot more important."

"This I gotta hear. What is it?"

Chip pulled a piece of paper out of his pocket and checked Pete's name off the list. Then, after extracting a promise of secrecy, he told Pete about Soapy's predicament. Pete was flabbergasted.

"Can't be! Why, why, it's impossible! Soapy Smith wouldn't steal a toothpick. What can I do to help?"

"I don't know, Pete. That's why I thought I would call a meeting of all of Soapy's friends to try to figure something out."

Pete nodded in approval. "That's what I call teamwork. Too many cooks don't *always* spoil the broth. You can count on me. Jimmy too! How about holding the meeting right here? We'll close at eleven o'clock and pull the blinds. OK?"

"Great! You tell Jimmy. I'll get word to everyone else."

"What about training rules? I thought you guys were s'posed to be home by eleven o'clock."

"I'll talk to Coach about it. I'll see you at eleven o'clock."

Chip left the restaurant and hurried down Main Street toward police headquarters. On the way he thought about the kind detective who had helped him straighten out some of Isaiah Redding's problems. Lieutenant Byrnes, director of University's Police Athletic League program, was a real friend of kids. Chip found the detective at his desk and plunged right into the problem. Byrnes knew Soapy and was generally familiar with the case. He listened attentively while Chip detailed Soapy's travels on the disastrous night.

"Detectives Parks and Minton have been giving him a pretty rough time."

"Smith is having quite an ordeal, Chip. But Fred and Gil are up against it too.

"You see, a detective is in a little different position than a police officer. Police officers are given regular assignments, called beats, and their duties are more or less routine whether they're walking or in a patrol car.

"Detectives may be assigned to certain types of cases. It's up to them to follow all leads, question suspects, set up the machinery of identification through fingerprinting, and question witnesses and all others who may have some knowledge of the case to help solve it. It's a tough and often dangerous job."

"I know, Lieutenant. Soapy realizes that too. But they've got him worried sick by the questioning and Welsh's identification."

Byrnes nodded. "That's understandable. Soapy's big difficulty is Welsh's identification of him. That puts Fred and Gil in a tight place. They can't take a single thing for granted. They have to follow through on every angle."

"But I've known Soapy all my life—"

"But they haven't, Chip."

"Well, I know that Soapy Smith couldn't do anything wrong."

"There again, Fred and Gil don't know that. The impossible seems to be the rule in many of the cases they solve. Some people who become involved in crime are unable to recall any part of it, as in cases of amnesia, temporary insanity, and all sorts of mental lapses. It could happen to Smith or—let me see the drawing."

Byrnes studied the drawing carefully. "Not bad," he said, tapping the paper with his finger. "We have a sketch artist who does the same thing when we have no photograph to go on. This isn't bad at all. What else are you doing?"

"That's about it. We did place an ad in the paper to find the guys who helped change Soapy's flat tire."

"Perhaps I can help. I'll ask Fred and Gil if it's OK to pass out some of these sketches around the neighborhoods and at our shift meetings."

That evening, when Soapy reported for work, Chip's plans were all set. He had a stack of photocopies of the sketches. And when Pete Thorpe and Jimmy Chung pulled down the restaurant blinds at eleven o'clock that night, it looked like a Valley Falls reunion. Biggie Cohen, Joel Ohlsen, Tug Rankin, Red Schwartz, Speed Morris, Soapy, and Chip made up the hometown guys, and Fireball Finley, Phil Whittemore, Pete Thorpe, and Jimmy Chung were their adopted members. Chip explained the purpose of the meeting and what had been done. Then he waited for suggestions.

Biggie smacked the table with his massive fist. "I ought to go out there and pin that mini mart guy's ears back," he said angrily, squaring his big shoulders. "I know it sounds silly and it's foolish, but that's the way I feel."

"How about setting up a night watch on some convenience type stores?" Schwartz asked.

"That's a thought," Fireball said quickly. "It gives me an idea too. Couldn't this Welsh guy have yelled cops-and-robbers and kept the money?"

"He's a strange man, Fireball," Chip said, smiling. "But I don't think he has that much imagination."

"Maybe not," Biggie said. "But in my book, a person who would identify an innocent person as a thief is capable of anything."

Red Schwartz ventured, "There's only a few places open after eleven o'clock, and we could easily cover them. This guy's bound to try another robbery. He must look for places that stay open late and hit them when they're deserted."

"How about talking to this Welsh?" Whittemore asked. "Maybe we could make him change his mind about Soapy."

"Parks and Minton wouldn't like that," Chip objected quickly. "Besides, it would probably only antagonize the man. Who knows what he would do if he thought we were trying to influence him."

"You can say that again," Soapy muttered.

At the conclusion of the meeting, Chip passed out copies of the sketch. They all agreed to help with the night watches. Chip would make the assignments. Then Pete served coffee "on the house," and Speed and Pete drove the Jeff crowd home.

Tuesday was the beginning of a long, hard week for Chip. Studying was especially difficult because Chip found it hard to concentrate. He staggered through though and then made up the watch lists. He also called on Lieutenant Byrnes. The detective was not very enthusiastic about the night-watch plan, but he gave Chip several emergency phone numbers to call and advised him not to play a policeman's role.

"The sketch idea is fine, Chip. But trying to catch a thief red-handed is something else. I admire your determination to help your friend, but it's dangerous. For the time being, I suggest you confine the watches to the places near the campus.

"If you or any of your friends see someone acting suspiciously, call one of the numbers I gave you and let us handle the situation. Try to get a good description of the man, his car, and the license plate number, and note the time. But let us do the rest. Remember, Chip, a man with a gun often loses his head. And when he does, well, someone usually gets hurt. Be sure to make it clear to the rest of your friends that they're merely trying to get information.

"Oh, I nearly forgot." He paused and smiled. "As you know, we patrol the campus area pretty carefully, so don't have your guys hiding in the bushes, or they may be considered suspicious themselves."

Chip took the Triangle Mini Mart watch that night. Biggie Cohen and Speed Morris were assigned to the convenience stores in nearby areas. Hopeful and excited, Chip slipped into the shadows across from the Triangle. But as the minutes ticked away and the cold wind bit through the coat he was wearing, his enthusiasm waned. It was a long, bitter evening. Few cars stopped at the station, and he breathed a sigh of relief when Welsh finally closed up and drove away.

Chip was out on his feet when he got home. Soapy was asleep, but the redhead was far from enjoying his slumber. He turned and tossed and murmured all night. Chip was up at five o'clock the next morning, hitting the books, preparing for his French test. Soapy joined him a little later and scarcely said a word. Both were concerned about their upcoming midterms.

When Chip limped into the locker room that afternoon, Murph Kelly greeted him grumpily. After he examined Chip's knee, he was grouchier than ever. "No practice for you," he said gruffly. "Now get out of here and don't come back until Friday noon."

That was a break for Chip. The sore knee and Soapy's trouble had taken his mind off his studies, and now that midterms were right around the corner, every minute he could devote to his books was important.

Red Schwartz, Jimmy Chung, and Joel Ohlsen covered the Wednesday and Thursday watches with no results. Pete Thorpe had been busy too. He had distributed the sketch copies to his friends around town. Chip waited expectantly, hoping the missing men would turn up. But nothing happened. And every day, as he watched Soapy's spirits drop, Chip became more determined.

Before it seemed possible, it was Friday, midterms were over, and it was nearly time for Chip to report for the two-day trip on which the team would meet its archrivals, A & M and Southern.

Chip waited for Soapy in the library, caught between two fires: loyalty to the team and a fierce desire to remain beside his buddy. But Soapy took care of that situation, setting Chip right.

"You can't let the team down, Chip. They need your help. And don't forget, A & M is the biggest game on the schedule. This year or any year. I know what you're thinking, Chip, and I appreciate it. But I can take care of myself. I just won't stand for you letting the team down because of me. Nothing is going to happen around here in two days that hasn't already happened."

Now, sitting on the table while Murph Kelly and Dr. Terring examined his knee, Chip half hoped he would be left behind. Then he saw his teammates' tense faces as they stood by, anxiously awaiting the verdict, and he knew Soapy was right. He belonged with the team.

"It doesn't look too bad," Dr. Terring said, turning to the trainer. "What do you think, Murph?"

Kelly shook his head uncertainly. "I don't know, Doc. You can't tell everything by palpating. We just have to go by what Chip tells us."

"That isn't very much," Terring concluded.

"But it always feels the same," Chip said quickly. "Whether I play or not. And the brace is wonderful. It holds my knee real tight."

"Sure," Kelly rasped. "Sure it does. Why wouldn't it?"

"I'll tell Coach when it's bothering me, Doc," Chip promised. "Word of honor."

"We've got to win these two games," Barkley said.

"He'll help just sitting on the bench," Andy Thornhill chimed in. "Right, guys?"

The responding chorus from the players left little doubt of their feelings, and Terring shook his head in resignation. "All right, Hilton. But I'm holding you to your promise. Remember, word of honor!"

CHAPTER 11

Truth Will Win Out

TRADITIONAL RIVALS and natural rivals are not always synonymous. But both terms meant the same thing to State and A & M. A victory in any sport meant a successful season and guaranteed that the coach of the winning team would be back for another season for either school.

A & M had won the conference title the previous year and was well on its way to a successful defense of the championship. The Aggies had won fourteen and lost only two games so far, and nine of the victories had been in conference competition. On the debit side of the ledger, there was nothing but a big goose egg.

The two-hundred-mile bus ride from University to Archton was not much of a trip. But most of the Statesmen were weary when they reached the A & M Hotel and Convention Center. After a light meal, Murph Kelly made the players rest in their rooms until game time.

HARDCOURT UPSET

When the Statesmen lined up against their arch-rivals at 8:30 that evening, they were fresh, confident, and determined to win. Chip sat out the first ten minutes as his teammates held their own, matching the Aggies point for point. But when A & M began to forge ahead to lead 26-20, Corrigan sent Chip in for Andy Thornhill. The A & M fans gave Chip a tremendous hand. But he couldn't do much. His knee was stiff, and before he could get going, the half ended with A & M leading 30-21.

Coach Corrigan tried to protect Chip again in the second half. But when A & M broke loose with a nine-point splurge to lead by fifteen points, he had no alternative but to try everything in the book. He revised his lineup and sent the Statesmen into their zone press.

The Aggies were ready for State's famous Holiday Tournament strategy, but they couldn't cope with the accurate shooting of Jimmy Chung, Speed Morris, Sky Bollinger, J. C. Tucker, and Chip Hilton. The wide-open scramble gave Chip more than enough time to get in position, and his long shots rippled the cords with deadly precision.

In the final seconds of the game, the Aggies assigned two men to play Chip all over the court. That left one man unguarded—it turned out to be Jimmy. The Statesmen located him immediately and hit the dribbling wizard with the ball. Jimmy was all alone under the basket when he scored the winning basket to put State ahead by one at the final buzzer, 72-71. Chip got twenty-eight points during the twenty-two minutes he played.

It was a great win for State, and the locker room celebration was reminiscent of the scene following the tournament victory. Chip felt good when he went to bed that night. But the next morning every step brought a streak of pain from his ankle to his thigh. He covered up as best he could and kept the pain to himself. Or at least he thought he did. But later, after the bus trip to Southern, Murph Kelly appeared in the room Chip was sharing with Speed and worked on his knee for nearly an hour.

"Who do you think you're kidding?" Kelly demanded. "Remember your promise."

"But it didn't hurt while I was playing."

"Just the same, if it isn't any better tonight, you tell Coach. You hear?"

As the gruff trainer banged the door behind him, Speed cast a long look in Chip's direction and then buried his nose back into his novel. "He's right, man. You watch that knee."

That night, while he was warming up, Chip saw Speed, Kelly, and Coach Corrigan watching him closely. He was on the bench when the game started, and he remained there all through the first half. It was a slow, control-ball contest, the type of game State's veterans handled best.

Ten minutes into the second half, Southern moved out in front and Coach Corrigan called for a time-out. "How about it, Chip? Are you all right?"

Chip leaped to his feet. "Sure! Yes, sir!"

Corrigan eyed him warily, then nodded. "All right. But you let me know. Report for Thornhill."

Corrigan's slow attack eliminated a lot of the sudden starts, stops, and change-of-direction slants State's pressure attack required, but Chip found the slow movements were more than he could maintain. But he kept trying and managed to score three three-pointers to put State two points ahead. Then, for the first time since his injury in the tournament, he said "uncle." He had gone as far as he could go.

As soon as State got the ball, Chip asked Barkley to call for a time-out. When the referee signaled, Chip walked slowly to the bench. "I'm sorry, Coach," he said. "I guess you had better take me out."

Murph Kelly sat down beside him and loosened the brace. "I'm glad you did the right thing," he growled.

State's veterans held the two-point lead, keeping the ball until they got their shots. They played a tight man-to-man defense and lasted it out. The final score: State 65, Southern 63.

The next morning, the bus took them back to University. It was three o'clock when they reached Jeff. Joel Ohlsen and Biggie Cohen saw Chip and Speed from the reading room and hurried out to help them with their bags. They were buzzing with excitement.

"The whole campus is talking about last night. Nice going! What an upset!"

"Where's Soapy?" Chip asked.

"He went out early this morning," Biggie told him, a frown darkening his face. "We've got to do something about this thing fast, Chip. It's really wearing him down."

"Any news?"

"Nope, not a thing."

"I'm going down to Pete's. If you see Soapy, tell him I'll wait there until six o'clock."

Jimmy Chung was already on the job when Chip reached the restaurant. He brought Chip a hot chocolate and the Sunday papers. "Locke again," he said tersely, opening the *News*. "Read that third paragraph."

Chip read the paragraph aloud. "'Lack of practice seems to have little effect upon the shooting accuracy of State's leading scorer, particularly on the team's road trips. This reporter attended four State practices this past week, and Chip Hilton was absent each time. It must be gratifying, even to a star of Hilton's magnitude, to relax during the strenuous practice sessions and then show up in time to star in the interesting road games.'"

"Well?" Jimmy demanded.

"I'm used to it, Jimmy."

"I'll never get used to that guy. Oh! Tech won again. Number thirteen. That's a lucky number."

"I guess it's about as lucky as unlucky. By the way, where's Pete?"

"He took off as soon as I came in."

"Anything new on the sketch?" Chip asked hopefully.

"Nothing much. Pete's been busy though. He's got that sketch plastered all over town."

Jimmy went back to work, and Chip opened the *Herald* to the sports section. There was a story about the Southern game on the first page and a schedule of the Marksmanship Tournament. Chip read both and then turned the page. A banner extended across the top of page two.

UNDEFEATED POLY-TECH RACKS UP
NUMBER THIRTEEN,
ENGINEERS EXTEND WINNING STREAK

A picture of the Tech varsity was smack in the center of the page, and a double-column story followed. Chip glanced at the picture, struck once more by the team's lack of height. *The biggest one isn't much taller than I am,* he marveled. *Not many teams go undefeated without a couple of big men.*

He studied the faces of the Tech stars and was engrossed in the picture when Soapy slipped into the booth bench across from Chip. One look at Soapy's worried face was enough for Chip. "What's the matter? Are you sick?"

Soapy shook his head. "Not the way you mean, Chip. But I'm sick enough, just the same."

"Why? What happened?"

"Plenty. Parks and Minton came to the store last night just as we were closing up and asked me if I'd mind taking a little ride with them." Soapy sighed. "Well, to make a long story short, I got in their car and we drove out to the mini mart. As if I didn't know where we were going. And when we got there, they put a hat on my head—it was brown this time.

"Then they gave me a blue sweater and told me to put that on and sit behind the wheel of their car. They took the keys out first, and then they asked me to get out and walk into the store and up to the counter."

"What happened then?"

"Well, Welsh takes one look at me and says—and these are his exact words—'It looks just like him! I told you it was him a week ago!'"

Soapy snorted contemptuously. "How about that?"

"How about that is right! Then what?"

"We drove back to Grayson's and went to Mr. Grayson's office. Then they told him about Welsh and asked me about a hundred times the same things they had already asked me a hundred times."

"How long did this go on?"

"Until about midnight."

"Didn't Mr. Grayson say anything?"

"Sure! When Parks told him about Welsh, Mr. Grayson said he wouldn't put any credence whatsoever in anything Welsh said. Then Parks said Welsh had made a positive identification, and Mr. Grayson said that he wouldn't take Welsh's word on a stack of Bibles as high as his desk.

"Then Mr. Grayson said he couldn't see how Welsh's latest identification had changed anything."

"What did Parks and Minton say to that?"

"Well, Minton said that he and Parks were on the spot because Welsh's boss had called the chief of police. That's why they took me out to the station and made me put on the hat and sweater.

"Then Mr. Grayson said he would call the chief of police the first thing Monday morning, that's tomorrow, and . . . Well, I guess that's it."

The two friends sat quietly for some time. Then Soapy broke the silence. "Parks and Minton think I'm guilty, Chip. I can tell by the way they act. What am I going to do?"

"Nothing," Chip said shortly. "You are innocent and it's up to them to find the guilty person. But, Soapy, maybe you should tell your parents about this, you know?"

Soapy's face took on a strength Chip had only seen a few times in his life. "I thought about it, Chip, but I decided that unless they actually charge me with something, I want to steel it out. You know my mom. She worries about everything, and there's nothing she can do about this anyway. And Dad—well, he's a great guy, but he'd get all upset, and that would make things worse on my mom. No, I'd like to leave them out of this for as long as I can. Besides, I've got you, right?"

Chip nodded firmly, and during the long silence that followed, began scribbling on a piece of paper, doodling idly. Then he began to sketch the face of the driver of the car who had helped with Soapy's tire.

Soapy watched him. "It's a perfect likeness. Right down to the last detail. The glasses even look the same."

HARDCOURT UPSET

"The glasses!" Chip said excitedly. "That's it! It's the glasses. Where's that paper?" He leafed impatiently through the *Herald*. "Here it is," he breathed.

Chip spread the paper out on the table and made several quick strokes on the page. "It could be."

"Could be what?" Soapy asked.

"Could be we've located your friend," Chip said, shoving the newspaper under Soapy's nose. "Recognize anyone?"

CHAPTER 12

A Shot in the Dark

"IT'S HIM!" Soapy cried excitedly. "I'm sure it's him! The glasses make the difference. He's the guy who changed the tire!"

"Maybe yes and maybe no," Chip cautioned. "Take it easy now. Don't jump the gun."

"What's his name?" Jimmy asked.

Chip ran his finger along the names below the picture. "Bill Sanders. He's the captain of the team."

"How about that!" Soapy said. "The captain of the Tech basketball team!"

"He'll be easy to find," Jimmy said. "Everybody on the Tech campus will know him."

"That's for sure," Chip said. "I'd better call Mr. Grayson."

"Let me call Mitzi first," Soapy said, rushing for the pay phone. "I promised her I'd call her first if something happened."

Seconds later, Soapy returned. "She's driving down. Right away! Going to drive us out there. Man, was she ever happy!"

"Don't count on it too much, Soapy," Chip warned. "It's just a shot in the dark."

"Uh-uh," Soapy said confidently. "It's him. It's gotta be him."

Chip called Mr. Grayson and told him about the picture and added that Mitzi was driving Soapy and him to the Tech campus.

"Fine, Chip," George Grayson said happily. "Be sure to let me know how you make out. Mrs. Grayson and I will be home all evening."

When Chip finished the call, Soapy and Jimmy were at the counter comparing the sketch with the photo in the newspaper.

"What a break," Jimmy said.

Soapy was on top of the world. "What do you mean break?" he demanded. "It wasn't a break! Chip did it foren—, uh, scien—, uh . . . efficiently."

"Well, forensically, scientifically, or efficiently," Jimmy retorted, "Pete and I will be waiting right here until you get back. Remember now, we'll be here if we have to stay open all night."

Several blasts of a car horn in front of the restaurant sent Soapy scurrying to the door. "C'mon, Chipper, it's Mitzi. See you later, Jimmy. We'll bring 'em back dead or alive!"

Tech was located in a small town five miles west of University. Mitzi covered the distance speedily and slowed the car down when the first 25 mph sign appeared, signaling they had reached their destination. "Now what?" she asked.

"We take a tour," Soapy said quickly. "The student union first, naturally. If we have no luck there, we hit a frat or a sorority, and, er—"

"Then we'll go to the dean's home," Chip added.

A SHOT IN THE DARK

They found the student union easily enough. And it was open. "Bill Sanders?" the girl sitting at a table near the door repeated, shaking her head. "Never heard of him, sorry."

"I know Bill Sanders," another girl at the next table offered. "Sure, I know him! He's the greatest basketball player in Tech history."

"Where can we find him?" Chip asked. "Do you know what dorm he's in?"

"Well, he lives in Addison Hall, but I know you can't find him right now. The team played in Chicago last night. Won again too! Thirteen straight now. I don't think the team is back yet."

"Do you know his phone number?"

"I can get it. There's a university directory at the information desk. Just a sec. I'll be right back." In just a few moments she was back with the precious phone number written on the back of a napkin. Chip tried calling, but there was no answer.

Back in the car, they paused to talk it over. Mitzi came up with the best suggestion. "Let's call Mr. Grayson. He'll know what to do."

"Good idea," Chip agreed. "We'll call from Pete's Place."

Back at University they stopped in front of the restaurant. Jimmy and Pete rushed out to the car. "Any luck?" Jimmy asked.

"No," Chip explained. "The team isn't in town."

Chip then called Mr. Grayson, who suggested they drive out to his home. "Bring Pete and Jimmy with you," he said.

Pete and Jimmy were enthusiastic when Chip told them about the invitation. "Let's go!" Pete said jubilantly. "I wouldn't miss any part of this if you *gave* me George Grayson's store."

George Grayson was one of University's wealthiest and most influential citizens. But it wasn't reflected in his mode of living and humble manner. Mrs. Grayson was the same type of person—sweet, unaffected, and friendly. They listened quietly while Chip related the events of the evening.

Later, while Mrs. Grayson was serving tea and cake, George Grayson excused himself and went into his den. Returning in a few minutes, he said, "I just talked to Dean Engle at Tech. He promised to have Bill Sanders in my office tomorrow morning at ten o'clock. Can you make it, Soapy?"

"Yes, *sir!* I sure can!"

"I'll be there too," Chip said firmly.

Chip didn't get much rest that night. Neither did Soapy. They both tried to conceal their restlessness from each other, breathing evenly and simulating sleep although both were wide awake. Soapy was the first to break. "All right!" he exploded abruptly, sitting up in bed and turning on his desk light. "Let's cut out the faking. So we can't sleep!"

"Right!" Chip agreed. "Let's talk."

George Grayson's office was overcrowded the next morning. Mr. Grayson sat behind his desk, and Parks and Minton sat with their backs to the picture window facing the front of the store. Chip and Soapy sat directly opposite the two detectives. The atmosphere was heavy and uneasy and ominously quiet, despite the steady tap-tapping of Ann Tracy's computer keyboard in the outer office.

Chip was extremely uncomfortable and wished someone would break the silence. Then the outside office door opened, and he heard Ann Tracy say, "Yes, he's expecting you. Go right in."

A SHOT IN THE DARK

Scarcely able to stand the suspense, Chip glanced over at Soapy. His lifelong friend was leaning forward, his legs bunched under his chair, every muscle in his body tense and ready. Then he leaped to his feet and rushed toward the broad-shouldered athlete who was framed momentarily in the door.

"Oh, man!" Soapy cried exultantly. "Am I glad to see you! Remember me?"

Soapy almost lifted the newcomer off the floor as he pulled him forward. Recognition dawned suddenly in Bill Sanders's eyes. "Hey!" he said, peering at Soapy through his glasses. "Sure! I remember you. You're the guy with the flat tire!"

There was no question about the recognition. Sanders shook hands with Soapy and then the redhead introduced Chip and Mr. Grayson and Gil Minton and Fred Parks. Sanders was obviously in the dark and, after the introductions, looked inquiringly at Soapy. "What's this all about? Dean Engle excused me from my classes and said—"

"Excuse me, Sanders, Soapy," Grayson said quickly. "Perhaps Mr. Parks and Mr. Minton can handle this better than anyone else."

Detective Parks took it from there, avoiding all reference to the robbery but making it clear that any information Bill Sanders could provide concerning the date, time, and place of the tire incident was of extreme importance to Soapy.

Sanders answered Parks's questions quickly and surely, and Gil Minton quietly entered each response in the familiar notebook. The date was unequivocally verified. Tech had played a home basketball game that Wednesday night, and Sanders and his two teammates, Stew Wilson and Ed Henry, were on their way to

University for something to eat when they saw Smith in the road.

Sure, he remembered the spot. He had made the drive between University and the Tech campus many times during his three and a half years in school. The time was somewhere between 11:30 and 11:45 because he and his two friends were in Burger King in University five minutes before closing time at midnight.

Then Minton took charge, and Parks jotted down the notes. Sanders told Minton that he remembered the basketball game was over at approximately 10:30 because his teammates remarked about the long game and noted the time while they were dressing.

He and his two teammates drove to their dorm, but they were in no mood to go to bed. Since curfew was canceled on game nights, they decided to drive to University to get something to eat.

Sanders was sure and precise with his answers. Detective Minton finished his questioning at last and glanced ruefully at Parks. "I guess that's it, Fred," he said, spreading his hands in a gesture of resignation. "What do you think?"

Parks shook his head slowly, whistling softly as he looked from Sanders to Soapy. He shrugged his shoulders and rose slowly to his feet. "Thanks, Sanders," he said, nodding to the tall athlete. "You've been a big help. Do you suppose we could locate Henry and Wilson without too much difficulty?"

"Sure. You'll find them at the student union cafeteria, the last table by the door, at twelve o'clock. Right on the dot. We meet there every day for lunch."

"Thanks. We'll drive over. Right now! Come on, Gil." At the door Parks paused. "Oh, yes. I'll call you at two o'clock, Mr. Grayson."

"I'll be here," Grayson replied shortly. "Two o'clock sharp." He turned to Sanders. "How about being my guest for lunch?"

"Excuse me, sir," Chip interrupted. "Pete is expecting Soapy and me for lunch. Bill might like to go along with us."

Grayson nodded. "I think that would be nice. Chip, would you drop back here at two o'clock?"

Lunch was waiting at the restaurant, and Jimmy and the jovial owner were eager to hear the details. Chip brought Bill Sanders up to date.

"That was some experience," Sanders said, shaking his head thoughtfully. "I wouldn't want to have those two men on my trail."

Chip left Soapy, Sanders, Jimmy, and Pete shortly before two o'clock and hustled back to Mr. Grayson's office. His employer was on the phone and gestured toward a chair when Chip entered.

It was the first time Chip had ever seen George Grayson angry. His employer's face was red, and his lips were pressed into a thin, determined line. He suddenly banged a fist on his desk, making the pen-and-pencil set jump. "This has gone far enough! By your own admission, Parks, the Tech players verified Smith's story. What's this *new* nonsense?"

George Grayson grew increasingly perturbed. "That's enough, Parks," he said sharply. "Why didn't you tell me about that this morning?" He listened intently, nervously tapping the desk with his fingers. "Nonsense! This is ridiculous."

He moved the telephone base roughly to the side of his desk and jammed the receiver down on the cradle. Then he leaned back in his chair and shook his head in disgust. "You'll never believe this, Chip. Parks now says the robbery could have taken place as much as twenty minutes earlier. The clock at the mini mart gains that much time every twelve hours. Hal Runyon—he's the owner—sets the clock himself each morning, and then the employees set it back from time to time during the day when they notice the discrepancy. No one remembers turning it back the day of the robbery."

CHAPTER 13

It's Not Just a Platitude

BILL SANDERS was laughing heartily when Chip glanced through the window of Pete's restaurant. Soapy was back in stride, and his audience was enjoying his performance. As worried and disheartened as he felt, Chip had to grin as he watched his pal's facial distortions and expansive gestures. Then the bad news he carried came down on him like the blow from a hammer, and his face sobered.

The levity ceased when Chip opened the door. "It's about time," Pete said. "What's the good word?"

"It isn't," Chip said grimly, sliding into the booth next to Soapy. Then he told them about the mini mart clock and the crew's forgetting to turn it back.

"How can they be sure they didn't?" Pete demanded. "Some memory!"

"That puts us right back where we started," Soapy groaned miserably.

"Maybe," Chip said. "Anyway, I've got to get going. I've got to see Murph Kelly and I'm late. Hang in there,

Soapy," Chip said as he gripped his friend's shoulder. "We're going to beat this thing. Count on it."

"I've got to leave too," Sanders said. "I've got a midterm first thing in the morning. Come on. I'll drop you and Jimmy off at Assembly Hall. It's right on my way."

Chip, Jimmy, and Bill got better acquainted on the short drive, and when they parted, the three boys had formed a new friendship.

"See you soon," Sanders said. "Happy hunting."

Murph Kelly was all alone when the two players reached the locker room. He greeted Chip sourly. "You shouldn't be here. After your treatment, beat it! And don't come back until Wednesday. I hope you're not figuring on playing against Western."

"I'm going to play if Doc will let me."

"We'll cross that bridge when we come to it," Kelly retorted.

Chip devoted the following day to his new plans. And that night, all of Soapy's friends were there. Chip had prepared a new watch list, and, encouraged by the success achieved through the sketch of Bill Sanders, Chip had made a drawing of the man Welsh had described, using Soapy as a model. A long discussion followed. Just before the meeting broke up, Chip gave them the revised watch list.

Dr. Terring put Chip through a long examination Wednesday afternoon and gave him permission to play. "Providing," he said pointedly, "you remember your word-of-honor promise."

Coach Corrigan used Chip sparingly in the game, playing him only a minute or two at a time. Nevertheless, he managed to get fourteen points, and the Statesmen squeezed through another toughie: State 73, Western 71.

IT'S NOT JUST A PLATITUDE

Chip's leg was so stiff after he finished his shower that he could scarcely make it up the steps to the main level. Speed brought his Mustang around front so Chip wouldn't have to walk any farther than the front door.

The next morning, every step was an effort, and he had a difficult time walking from one classroom to the next. Later, when he hobbled into the training room, Kelly hit the ceiling. "I knew it! Now you sit right where you are until I get back."

The trainer stormed out of the room, slamming the door behind him. In a few minutes he was back with Coach Corrigan and Dr. Mike Terring. "See for yourself," he said testily. "It's swollen up again. You'd better lay him off for a good rest. If you don't, he isn't going to be worth a dime when you need him most—against Brandon and A & M."

"Right!" Coach Corrigan said decisively.

Dr. Terring gave the knee a thorough examination, wiggling it from side to side and checking the knee's lateral stability. Then he took a basketball schedule out of his pocket. He studied it thoughtfully, pulling at his chin and mumbling under his breath. "Let's see. You play Midwestern here Saturday night, and Cathedral and Wesleyan away on the eleventh and twelfth. The next game is with Brandon on February 19.

"This is the third. I say he should have two weeks' rest—"

"Wait a second!" Chip interrupted. "Nothing doing! No, sir! Why, the season will be practically over—"

"Be quiet, Chip," Kelly said quietly.

Dr. Terring continued thoughtfully, "That will bring him up to the seventeenth, and he will probably be ready to play against Brandon on the nineteenth."

"Good!" Kelly cried. "How about the treatments?"

"I'm going to prescribe an anti-inflammatory. We'll skip everything else for a week," Terring said decisively. "Give the knee a complete rest." He turned to Chip. "Now I don't want you to do any practicing or running or anything else until February 17. That's an order."

The days passed quickly. It was a relief to have nothing to do in the afternoons except study. But as the days passed and nothing happened on the night watches, Chip began to think that his plans were a little on the foolish side. But he wasn't going to quit.

Jim Locke took a few potshots at Chip in the *News,* but Soapy's trouble had taken the edge off of the sportswriter's sarcastic quips. Chip scarcely gave them a thought. Saturday night, he sat on the bench and watched State slip past Midwestern in the last twenty seconds to win another close game, 67-66.

Sunday, back in his room after church, Chip settled himself comfortably on his bed and read the papers. Soapy had gone out on an errand, but he had opened the *News* to the sports pages, and Jim Locke's column was again marked in red. Chip anticipated something personal, but he was wholly unprepared for the shocker he found.

Chip Hilton, the defending champion, Sky Bollinger, the runner-up, and Bitsy Reardon, another strong contender, are local entries in the National Marksmanship Tournament scheduled for next Friday and Saturday, February 11-12.

Hilton's ailing knee has conveniently placed him on the "ex-athletics" list, and he will undoubtedly be present for the opening ceremonies. It will be interesting to see what Bollinger and Reardon will come up with to insure their participation in the tournament while State's basketball team is on the road.

IT'S NOT JUST A PLATITUDE

Chip read the paragraph several times, mulling it over in his mind. Then he picked up the *Herald*.

Bill Bell presented a picture of the conference situation in his column and drew attention to the race between Western, A & M, and Brandon for leadership.

Chip studied the standing of the teams. State was in fourth place and likely to stay there.

	CONFERENCE STANDINGS	
Teams	*Won*	*Lost*
Brandon	18	3
A & M	15	3
Western	14	3
State	17	6

The Tech record of fifteen victories and no defeats was featured in a separate paragraph, and Bell gave the Engineers an outside chance for district representation should the conference contenders weaken in their down-the-stretch drive.

The second sports page of the *Herald* was devoted to the Marksmanship Tournament. Entry lists and photographs of the leading contenders from both the state and the nation filled the page. Chip's picture was prominently featured. He laid the *Herald* aside and reread the second paragraph of Locke's column in the *News*.

"Soapy is right," he murmured. "Locke never gives up."

Chip remained close to Jeff the rest of the day, hitting the books and trying to keep Jim Locke out of his thoughts. Soapy joined him later, aware of Chip's feelings but thoughtfully silent, and the two buddies spent the evening studying. Around ten o'clock, they took a long walk. When they returned to Jeff, they went to bed but not to sleep.

Soapy was conjuring up a dream in which Jim Locke swam in the middle of a big lake filled with black ink. The writer struggled vainly like a fly caught on a piece of sticky flypaper.

"Now stew in your own juice," Soapy muttered.

"What?"

"Nothing, Chip. I was just daydreaming."

Chip tossed and turned all night. But when he got up Monday morning, he had reached an important decision. He was going to see Bill Bell and drop out of the tournament.

Bill Bell had just finished his work when Chip arrived at the sports office. He greeted Chip with a smile and waved to the chair beside his desk. "Sit down, Chip. How are you? What brings you around here?"

Chip took a deep breath. "I want to drop out of the tournament, Mr. Bell."

"Drop out?"

"Yes, sir. It isn't fair to the team."

Bill Bell pushed his chair back from the desk and leaned forward to face Chip. "I don't understand. Why isn't it fair to the team?"

"A lot of people think I'm using my knee as an alibi so I can practice my shooting."

"A lot of people? Nonsense! Every intelligent person in this town knows that Dr. Terring decides when a player is able to play."

Chip nodded uncertainly. "But Sky Bollinger and Bitsy Reardon told me they were going to drop out."

"That's a little different, Chip. In the first place, you're the defending champion and you have a bye until the fourth of March. Bollinger and Reardon are not eligible for byes, as you know. They have to qualify in the state. And, naturally, since the state trials take place when your team has away games, they have no alternative.

"You're in a different position. You don't have to compete in the state. It doesn't make any difference, as far as your position in the tournament is concerned, whether you make the trip or not." Bell paused and eyed Chip patiently. "You understand that, don't you, Chip?"

Chip nodded. "Yes, sir, but not many people know that."

"They will," Bell said grimly. "Now, Chip," he continued understandingly, "I know exactly how Jim Locke's sniping has affected you. I imagine you are familiar with the old saying: 'Sticks and stones may break my bones, but names will never hurt me.'"

Bell smiled and eyed Chip quizzically. Then he continued significantly, "Doesn't that apply to Jim Locke and the exaggerated, sensationalized opinions he prints in his column?"

"I guess so."

"All through life, Chip, an individual faces situations that provide the opportunity to choose the hard way or the easy way. Right now your road is a little rough. But I'm betting on you. And I seldom make a mistake when my estimate is based on character.

"Oh, yes. One more thing. A fighter never quits and a quitter never wins. It's not just a platitude, Chip. Think it over!"

CHAPTER 14

The Dean's List

AS SOON AS Chip left, Bill Bell picked up the phone and called Coach Henry Rockwell at the State University basketball office. The conversation was brief enough, but it accomplished its purpose. At any rate, Bell was smiling when he hung up. That night Chip was pleasantly surprised when his old high school coach walked into Grayson's stockroom.

"Hello, Chip," Rockwell said, sitting down at the desk. "Are you busy?"

"No, Coach. Not at all."

"Good. I thought I'd drop in and say hello. By the way, you seem to make Jim Locke's column about every day. He must be a friend of yours."

Chip grinned in return. "I don't think so," he said lightly.

Rockwell changed the subject. "What's wrong with Soapy, Chip? Is he in some sort of trouble?"

Chip told Coach Rockwell about Soapy's problem and

the steps he and the rest of Soapy's friends were taking to clear him.

"I knew there was something wrong. Is there anything I can do?"

"I don't think so, Coach. Not right now anyway."

"Well, you know where to reach me. I'm sure it will work out all right. But, if it goes any further, call me. Better yet, maybe we'll call Speed's father. Never hurts to have an attorney in your corner—especially a man of integrity like Bull Morris." Rockwell hesitated, studied Chip searchingly for a second, and then continued gently. "By the way, I hope you're not letting Jim Locke get under your skin."

Chip shook his head. "It doesn't mean a thing, Coach."

"Good! I knew you were too smart to let that bother you. And I'm glad to see you're taking care of that knee. That reminds me. I talked to Doc Jones on the phone this morning. He told me everyone at home is pulling for you to retain your shooting championship. I told him that went for Coach Corrigan, the team, and me too. Well, I guess I'll be getting along."

Later that night, when Chip and Soapy arrived at Pete's Place, Jimmy Chung greeted them with a long face. "Tech got beat tonight," he announced glumly. "Eighty-one to eighty."

"Heard it on the radio," Pete added. "Announcer said it was a rough game. Said there was some kind of a ruckus but didn't give any details. I guess we'll hear about it tomorrow night. Sanders said they would be over about ten o'clock."

"Do you think this will hurt their chances for the NCAA?" Jimmy asked.

"It shouldn't," Fireball said. "The game was played on the Brandon court, and that was a ten-point advantage. A one-point defeat is nothing to be ashamed of against a team like Brandon. Right, Chip?"

"Right! But I bet Bill Sanders is feeling low right now, though. I don't feel too good myself."

"Well," Soapy said, summing it up, "there's one thing for sure. There's no way Jim Locke can blame Chip for the defeat. C'mon. Let's go home."

The Thursday issue of the *Herald* played up the tournament, displaying pictures of the contestants and personal stories of their accomplishments. Bill Bell ran a small photo of Chip in his column and devoted the first paragraph to a description of Chip's knee injury. Then he explained how Dr. Mike Terring had sidelined Chip for ten days and that the marksmanship champion would not accompany the team on the road trip as a result.

Bell deplored Tech's first defeat but asserted that the Engineers had lost little stature in the one-point defeat. He pointed out that few teams ever went through a season undefeated. Always a student of history, Bell recalled Coach Bob Knight's great 1976 Indiana University team that established a monumental 32-0 record.

In the last paragraph, Bell cast the Statesmen in the role of spoilers, citing the importance of the Brandon game at Brandon University on February 19, the home game on March 2, and the final game of the season against A & M on March 7 at Assembly Hall. Victories in these three games, Bell claimed, might knock both teams out of the race for the conference honors and push Tech right into the tournament as the sectional representative.

Both Chip and Soapy were tired when they dropped into Pete's Place that night. But they forgot their own troubles when they saw Bill Sanders, Stew Wilson, and Ed Henry. Sanders was talking heatedly to Pete and

Jimmy and waited for Chip and Soapy to get settled. Then he banged the table and continued. "Sure!" he said. "That's exactly the way they play. And they get away with it!"

"They sure do!" Stew Wilson said vehemently. "You'll find out! They send one of their three big men into the pivot in rotation, and each one of them uses the same technique." He leaped to his feet to demonstrate the play.

"Look!" Stew said, leaning back against Chip and forcing him against the side of the booth. "You see what I mean?"

Chip grinned. "I see all right."

Then Ed Henry got into the act, replacing Wilson. He put all his weight against Chip and held his position. Then he pretended to catch a ball. "Now watch! Watch my elbow!" He raised his left elbow until it was level with Chip's eyes and turned, banging it up against Chip's face. Then he simulated a shot at the basket with his right hand. "Nice trick, huh?"

"Don't see how they can get away with that," Soapy said.

Stew Wilson pushed Ed Henry away. "That's nothing!" he said. "How about this?"

"Hold it!" Chip protested, lifting his hands in defense and laughing. "I believe you. Honest!"

"That's only a sample, Chip," Sanders said. "They fouled when they backed into us, all right, but the real business was the bang in the face."

"They never missed the shot either," Stew added dourly. "It was a perfect one-two."

"Then the official would call a foul on one of *us*," Ed Henry said.

"Yeah," Sanders added dryly. "For being stupid enough to stand still and get hit. Wonderful!"

"Don't worry," Stew Wilson said quietly. "We'll take care of *them*. This Saturday. They won't pull that stuff on the officials we have around here."

"Right!" Henry added bitterly. "Our officials call the games according to the rules."

"I can't wait," Wilson said quietly. "If there was ever a team I wanted to beat—"

"Don't get us wrong, guys," Sanders interrupted. "We're not angry because they broke our winning streak. That hurts, but losing is only a small part of it. The real travesty, as far as we're concerned, is that they didn't win fairly. That's why we're hot."

"We wouldn't tell this to anyone at Tech," Ed Henry said. "It's not an excuse. We're telling you guys because we know you won't repeat it."

"That's right," Sanders added, his face lighting up with a grin. "I guess we're just trying to get it out of our systems."

"That's what friends are for," Chip said. "We'll sure be pulling for you Saturday night."

Chip was wrong about that. All the support in the world wouldn't have helped Tech Saturday night because Brandon canceled the game. The Brandon University president made the decision because of the intense feelings shown between the teams during and immediately following the game at Brandon.

So Chip's three Tech friends were with him both Friday and Saturday night when the sectional contenders competed for marksmanship positions. Sanders, Wilson, and Henry were upset, bitter because of Brandon's cancellation, but they didn't say much about it. Chip was quiet, too, annoyed by the attention the reporters and photographers were giving him. But they were all elated when they watched the news and learned that State had defeated Cathedral, 80-79, Friday night. And State beat Wesleyan by two, 63-61, Saturday afternoon.

Soapy was propped up in bed and trying to study when Chip reached Jeff. The redhead closed the book and tossed it on the floor. But he grinned cheerfully, trying to cover up the tired, worried lines etched on his face. "Just can't concentrate, Chip," he said wryly.

Chip couldn't concentrate either. And that was serious. Chip and Soapy were working while going to school, and they couldn't afford to let anything interfere with the time they set aside for studying.

The next morning Soapy got the Sunday papers. But when he opened the *News* to the sports pages and started to read Jim Locke's column aloud, Chip held up a hand to silence him. "Hold it, Soapy. I want to tell you something."

"What?"

"I'm not going to read anything Locke writes until after basketball season ends, and I don't want you to tell me about anything he puts in his column."

"Why?"

"Because I don't want to think about the things he writes. Isn't that sensible? If I don't know what he writes, it can't bother me."

Soapy nodded his head slowly. "Sure," he said thoughtfully, "that's a good idea." He tossed the *News* aside and picked up the *Herald.*

"What's in the *Herald?*" Chip asked.

"I thought you just said you weren't going to read the papers?"

"Not the papers—just the *News* and Locke's column."

Soapy grinned. "I was just asking! Well, you hit Bill Bell's column. He says the team will have a week of rest, and by the time State meets Brandon, you'll be back in playing condition. And listen to this: 'Tech continues as the outstanding candidate to represent this section in the NCAA championships.' Sounds good, right?"

"It sure does. If any team ever deserved the honor, it's Tech. I don't think any team made up of students, and I mean *students,* ever made a record like theirs. Besides, they're great guys."

"And then some," Soapy said in admiration. "Imagine! Every player on the team is on the Dean's List. That's really something in an engineering school."

"You're right about that," Chip agreed.

The days passed quickly enough. Chip put Jim Locke out of his mind and concentrated on his books and the night watches. And, with the improvement of his knee, the old basketball urge returned. Wednesday afternoon, the day before he was to report back to practice, Chip showed up at Grayson's with his basketball shoes.

"Where do you think you're going?" Mitzi queried.

"Over to the Y," Chip said calmly. "I'm going to see if my knee is as good as it feels."

Chip had no difficulty getting the use of a ball and permission to practice a few shots. His knee felt fine, and he became so absorbed with his practice shots that he didn't even notice the spectators who were watching his marksmanship. One observer stared at Chip incredulously and then, grinning delightedly, hurried away. Jim Locke wanted to see Jim Corrigan before writing his next column.

CHAPTER 15

Secret Practice

MURPH KELLY groaned and jerked his head toward the far end of the court. "Oh, oh!" he groaned. "Here comes trouble, Coach. I guess I'd better find some unfinished business."

Corrigan waited uncomfortably as Jim Locke approached. The young coach exerted every bit of his willpower to conceal the dislike he felt for this reporter. He was prepared for the usual probing, baiting, and caustic questioning.

"Hello, Corrigan," Locke said abruptly. He then pounced: "I thought Hilton was supposed to be resting his leg."

"He is."

"That's what you think!"

"I don't understand—" Corrigan, puzzled, was cautious. He knew Locke had something up his sleeve, and he wanted to tread easily.

"He's been practicing for Bill Bell's shooting promotion at the Y."

Corrigan shook his head. "I don't follow you."

"You mean you don't or you won't—"

"I mean I don't know what you're talking about," Corrigan said curtly. "If you don't mind, Locke, I've got to get on with practice. Excuse me."

"I don't mind," Locke said slyly. "I just thought you ought to know about your injured star's extracurricular basketball activities. You see, Mike Terring told me that Hilton was to rest his leg until Thursday, February 17, and, well, that's tomorrow."

Corrigan nodded. "Yes, that's right."

"Well, then, how come he was practicing at the Y? Did he have your permission?"

"No—no, he didn't."

"What are you going to do about it?"

"I don't expect to do anything about it until I know all the circumstances."

"But isn't it the same as breaking training? And isn't it disloyal to the team to practice secretly for—let's say— Bell's shooting tournament instead of practicing with the team and trying to win games for State?"

"I can't answer that, Locke," Corrigan said slowly, turning away. "You'll have to excuse me now. I've got work to do."

Just about the time Jim Locke was talking to Coach Corrigan, Chip was finishing his little workout at the Y. He was pleased with the condition of his knee and imbued with a tremendous urge to get back with the team. His good spirits carried over to the next day and right up to the moment he entered the locker room. Then he got a slight shock. Murph Kelly's reception was frosty.

"Coach wants to see you, Hilton," Kelly said dourly. "He's in his office."

Chip loped upstairs and in through the double doors of

the basketball office. Boxes of basketballs, readied for Coach Corrigan's autograph, were stacked up against a filing cabinet, and plaques and photographs of NCAA coaches and former players practically covered every inch of wall space. Marianne Woods, one of the secretaries, smiled ruefully and nodded her head in the direction of Corrigan's office. "Coach is waiting for you. Go right in, Chip."

Coach Corrigan was sitting at his desk when Chip knocked on the open door. "Come in and sit down, Chip," he said slowly. "How's your knee?"

"It's fine, Coach. I sure hope Doc Terring will let me practice." Chip waited uncertainly, sensing that something was wrong.

"That's what I wanted to talk about. Are you sure you've been following Doc's orders?"

"Why, yes, Coach. Sure."

"Then you haven't been practicing on your own?"

"No, sir. Not a bit except a little shooting at the YMCA yesterday afternoon." Chip paused and eyed Corrigan uncertainly. "I didn't do a bit of running, Coach. I took maybe forty or fifty easy shots at the basket, that's all. Was that wrong, sir?"

"I don't exactly know, Chip. Have you seen the *News* today? Jim Locke's column?"

Chip grinned slightly. "No, sir, I haven't been reading Mr. Locke's column for some time."

"That's not a bad idea," Corrigan mused. "Think I'll try it myself." He shoved a newspaper clipping across the desk. "Read that."

STATE STAR HOLDS SECRET PRACTICE
SPORTS ESPIONAGE

Many years ago when I was a freshman in college, rival college athletic departments often boasted an efficient sports espionage system. Various emissaries ventured forth in appropriate disguises to seek out the top-drawer secrets of their respective rivals. This development led to counterespionage practices, such as posting security guards and holding secret team workouts behind closed gates and doors.

ETHICS

Inevitably, however, a code of ethics did away with the spying techniques, and today rival spies (scouts) are welcomed at various games and given choice seats from which to secure their information. The above was brought to mind yesterday afternoon when I learned about an unusual type of practice session at the University YMCA.

SIDELINED STAR

Local basketball fans are aware that Chip Hilton, State's high-scoring basketball star, has been sidelined by Dr. Mike Terring for the past few games. Hilton was excused from team practices with specific orders to rest his knee until Dr. Terring gave it a thorough examination. *That examination is scheduled for this afternoon.*

SECRET PRACTICE

However, this column received an eyewitness report that Hilton has been practicing his national marksmanship championship shots in secret practices at the local YMCA.

LOYALTY

Since Chip Hilton is a vital member of the State team, which has been desperately and vainly battling for a position in the all-important conference standings, the information came as a shock! We have always believed

that team sports are justifiable, primarily because of the
development of loyalty to team and school.

COACH IN THE DARK

State's hoop coach, Jim Corrigan, was informed
of Hilton's secret workouts just yesterday afternoon.
Corrigan said that Hilton did *not* have his permission
to engage in such practices.

"Oh, Coach," Chip said lamely, shaking his head, "I
never dreamed I was doing anything wrong."

"I know," Corrigan said empathetically. "You're sure
you practiced just the one time?"

"I'm positive, Coach, and I'm sorry. I guess there isn't
anything else I can say."

Corrigan smiled. "That's all you need to say. Forget
it. Now you go and see Doc Terring. I'll call him and
explain everything. I'll tell Kelly too."

Murph Kelly was just hanging up the receiver when
Chip reached the locker room. He glanced at Chip and
shook his head. "That guy causes more trouble than the
mumps," he growled disgustedly. "Locke, I mean," he
added belligerently. "C'mon. We gotta see Terring. He's
not at the med center. He's in his office here."

Dr. Terring smiled wryly when Kelly and Chip
arrived in his office. "Coach just called," he said. "I guess
the less said the better. Let's have a look at that knee."

Later, Chip followed Murph Kelly back to the locker
room and quickly changed for practice. "I'm glad Coach
wasn't upset, Murph," he said happily.

"No thanks to Jim Locke," Kelly growled.

When Chip reached the court, practice was underway. But that meant nothing to the Statesmen when they
saw Chip. They stopped right in the middle of one of

Corrigan's drills and surrounded him, their enthusiasm wholeheartedly and joyously expressed.

"How do you feel, Chipper? Now you take it easy."

"Hope you haven't been paying any attention to those stories in the *News*."

"Who does that jerk think he's kidding?"

"Right! Wonder what makes him think we don't want you to win the marksmanship tournament?"

"You *gotta* win it now. Just to show him up."

"Forget Locke. Bill Bell's a better writer anyway."

"Whoever said Locke could write?"

Coach Corrigan's whistle broke up the discussion, and Chip and Murph Kelly walked down to the practice basket to limber Chip up. The trainer worked Chip for half an hour, his keen eyes studying Chip's every move. He then dismissed him.

"See you tomorrow afternoon, Chip. Now get out of here and take care of that knee."

Chip worked out again Friday afternoon, and when the State basketball squad assembled at Assembly Hall that night for the trip to Brandon University, he was there. Soapy, Bill Sanders, Stew Wilson, and Ed Henry were also there to see the team off, and Chip introduced the Tech stars to his teammates.

"We think you can take them," Sanders told his new State friends, "but you'll have to stop their big men under the boards. They're plenty tough."

Coach Jim Corrigan had been a quiet listener. Now he entered the conversation. "How do you think a collapsing zone would work?" he asked.

"Good!" Sanders said enthusiastically. "You've got the height and the weight to give them a battle under the boards. We just don't have any really big men. That's why we didn't try it."

SECRET PRACTICE

"We've got them, and we'll try it," Corrigan said grimly. "Thanks for your help, Sanders."

Coach Corrigan followed Sanders's advice the following night and used a 2-3 zone, floating all five defensive players back under the basket to counter Brandon's over-sized forward line. And it worked. Brandon's board attack was held in check, and that equalized control of the ball.

It was a tight, bitter contest. Brandon was up for the game, grimly determined to win, fighting for the conference championship. Perhaps State's aggressive under-the-boards game rattled Brandon. At any rate, the lead changed hands twenty-seven times during the forty minutes of play. Coach Corrigan kept Chip on the bench until the last three minutes of the game. Then, with a minute to play and Brandon leading, 77-75, it was Chip's baby jumper which enabled State to tie the score.

Brandon held the ball for one shot and took it with ten seconds left. But it spun around and around the rim and then out, and Sky Bollinger's elbows were practically on the hoop when he took the rebound. He turned in the air and fired the ball three-quarters of the way upcourt to Speed Morris. Speed pegged the ball to Jimmy Chung. Jimmy could have taken the shot, but he turned in the air and whipped the ball back to Chip near midcourt.

Chip barely had time to aim the ball and let it fly. As it left his hands, the horn ended the game. But it couldn't stop the ball as it arched gracefully and swished through the rim and the net to win the game for State by a score of three, 80-77.

The Statesmen were almost delirious with joy, went after Chip, and tried to get him up on their shoulders. "Yea, Chip! What a shot!"

"Come on, guys," Chip pleaded. "Cut it out. It was a lucky heave."

But they wouldn't let him go. Chip pulled and twisted away, and then he felt the pain. It streaked up his leg like a flash of lightning. Murph Kelly was trying to fight his way to Chip's side, but he was too late. The next morning, when the Statesmen boarded the team bus for their return to State, Chip was limping badly. But he joined in the happy chattering of his teammates.

"That makes it twenty and six, guys," Barkley cried. "We've still got a chance."

"Gotta take all of them," King warned.

"We'll take 'em," Gowdy said confidently. "Chip's back, and that's all we need."

Soapy and the Tech crowd met the bus when it pulled into University Sunday afternoon. Sanders, Wilson, and Henry shook hands delightedly with every player on the squad. "Man, what a victory!" Sanders cried. "You guys sure squared things for us with Brandon."

"We owe you some thanks, Sanders," Coach Corrigan said gratefully. "Maybe we can do it again on March 2. We'll sure try."

Soapy had Speed's Mustang, and on the way to Jeff, he insisted Speed and Chip tell him all about the great win. Speed obliged while Chip listened, pleasantly relaxed, his knee forgotten. He was actually half-asleep when Soapy pulled into a parking spot right behind Jeff. Chip got out and followed his friends up the walk, determined to take a nap as soon as he reached his room.

But Chip came to life with a start when he reached the first-floor hallway. Detectives Gil Minton and Fred Parks were waiting just inside the door.

Chip dropped his bag. "Now what?"

"Just waiting for Smith, that's all, Hilton," Minton answered quietly.

"Is there something new?" Chip asked, now fully

aware of the implications possible with the detectives' presence at Jeff on a Sunday.

"We think so," Parks said significantly. "Anyway, another convenience store was held up last night."

"By a redheaded guy about Smith's size," Minton added.

CHAPTER 16

The Test of a Man

"HERE WE go again," Soapy groaned, looking helplessly at Chip. "This is getting monotonous."

"We don't exactly think it's the most exciting case in history," Parks said dryly. "Where can we talk?"

"We can go into the library," Chip said. "There's probably no one there right now."

"I think I'll go on upstairs, Chip," Speed said, picking up the bags. "Want me to do anything? Maybe call my father?"

"I don't think so, Speed. Let's give it a little more time. I'll see you later."

Jefferson Hall's library, really a study room, consisted of a dozen tables and approximately fifty chairs. Chip led the way to a table in a corner of the room. "You don't mind if I stay, do you?"

"I guess not," Parks said. He tossed his notebook across the table to Minton. "You jot down the notes, Gil, and I'll ask the questions."

Minton dated a page. "All set, Fred."

Parks faced Soapy. "Now, Smith, where were you last night about 11:30?"

"I—I was watching the Triangle Mini Mart. Jimmy Chung made the trip with the team, and I took his place." Soapy hesitated, cleared his throat, and then continued uncertainly, "Chip and I and some of the other guys have been trying to—"

"We know you've been trying to play cops-and-robbers," Parks said impatiently. "Go on."

"Well, that's all," Soapy said, shrugging his shoulders."

"What time did you reach this watching place?"

"It was exactly eleven o'clock."

"Was anyone with you?"

"No, sir."

"How do you know it was eleven o'clock?"

"Well, I left Pete's Place at 10:45, and the Triangle clock showed eleven o'clock when I reached the gate across the street. And it showed twelve o'clock when Welsh closed up."

"Do you know where the City Service Station is?"

"Sure. I go past it two or three times every day."

"How long do you think it takes to walk from the City Service Station to the Triangle Mini Mart?"

Soapy shook his head. "I don't know, Mr. Parks. I haven't any idea."

"Did anyone see you on watch?"

"I don't think so."

"Then all we have is your word that you were across from the Triangle Mini Mart from eleven o'clock until Welsh closed at twelve. Right?"

"I guess so."

"All right, Smith," Parks said, rising to his feet, "suppose we ride down to the City Service Station and talk to the man who was on duty last night. We asked him to meet us there."

Chip had never felt so helpless in his life. There hadn't been a thing he could say or do to help Soapy. All he could do right now was stick with Soapy and see it through. "Do you mind if I go along, Mr. Parks?" he asked.

Parks glanced at Minton. "How about it, Gil?"

Minton pondered a brief second and then shook his head. "I don't think so, Fred. It's just a matter of identification. Smith will be right back if he's in the clear. Otherwise, we can call Hilton."

"I'll be right here," Chip said grimly, turning to Soapy. "Don't worry."

Soapy nodded and forced a grin. "Imagine! Another guy with freckles and red hair who looks like me! Unbelievable, Dr. Watson. Unbelievable! Well, let's go."

It was a long hour. Speed, Biggie, Joel, and Red all crammed in Chip and Soapy's room and waited impatiently. Speed strode restlessly back and forth, from one end of the room to the other, pausing each time at the window to look down the street. "Suppose this guy identifies Soapy," he said worriedly. "Then what?"

"He won't," Chip said confidently. "It just isn't possible."

"It was possible with Welsh," Red said quickly.

"There couldn't be another guy like Welsh," Chip said.

"One thing is for sure," Biggie said. "There's a guy somewhere in this town who looks like Soapy. And I mean *really* looks like him."

"Unless he wears a wig," Chip said, grinning. "Hey," he continued thoughtfully, "maybe he does! It sounds silly, I know, but there's got to be some reason no one has seen this guy."

"Here they are!" Speed said excitedly. "Soapy's

getting out of the car. Alone! And Parks and Minton are driving away."

Chip was the first one out of the room and running down the stairs, but he didn't have much of a lead. They all met Soapy just as he opened the street door, overwhelming him with questions.

"What happened?"

"Is everything all right?"

"What did he say?"

"Did he identify you?"

"Hey! One at a time," Soapy cried. "Anyway, there wasn't much to it. The man at City Service Station said the holdup guy was about my size and had red hair, but he didn't think I was the one who robbed him. Man, did Parks and Minton take *that* hard! They asked him a lot of questions, but they couldn't get anything else out of him. What a life!"

Dr. Mike Terring would not be swayed. "No, sir! You're not practicing and you're not playing. You're going to rest that knee—for a week."

"But, Doc, we've still got a chance for the conference title."

Terring grinned. "With a twenty and six record? Not a chance."

"But if we win all the rest, Doc, we'll end up with a twenty-four and six record. That's an eighty-percent average. We can *win!*"

"Sure!" Kelly said scathingly. "Sure we can! All we have to do is ask A & M, Brandon, and Western to lay down and play dead. Nothing to it!"

"It's possible, Murph," Dr. Terring said.

"I've got to play," Chip said. "We've got to beat A & M and Brandon."

"Yeah," Kelly said. "It's a matter of life or death."

"It means a lot to me," Chip countered.

"I know, Chip," Dr. Terring said kindly. "I'm sorry, but I'll have to order you to stop all basketball activity for a week. Until next Monday. Then we'll talk about Brandon and A & M."

It was a tough blow. Chip took Dr. Terring's orders literally and didn't even watch the practices. He went directly to work after his classes and took his turn on the night watches. About the only ray of sunshine was the regular and loyal reporting of Soapy's friends for their scheduled night watches.

Friday and Saturday brought the final and disastrous blow to State's conference championship hopes. Carlton defeated the Statesmen, 56-54, on Friday night, and Riordon topped them, 51-49, on Saturday night. Pete was talking to the Tech crowd when Chip and Soapy arrived after work.

"Hi ya, Chip, Soapy," Pete said glumly. "I guess we can hang up our shoes now. Right?"

"Not yet!" Chip said.

Pete shrugged. "I don't get it. What's left?"

"Brandon and A & M," Soapy replied. "Beating A & M is as good as winning the championship."

"And are we ever pulling for you to beat Brandon again!" Bill Sanders said fervently.

"We'll kill 'em!" Soapy growled. "Chip will be back Monday."

"To see Doc Terring," Chip corrected.

"You'll play," Soapy said confidently.

Stew Wilson thumped his fist on the table. "You can knock 'em both out of the championship. Brandon and A & M."

"Don't forget Western," Sanders reminded him.

"A & M, Brandon, and Western all have identical records. Twenty and four with one game left to play. If State can beat Brandon and A & M, and Western loses to Southern, it will throw the conference into a three-way tie."

"And put Tech in the national championships," Soapy added. "*That* would make *everybody* in this town happy."

"It's too much to ask for," Sanders said lightly. "Come on. I'm going home. I'll drop you guys off at the dorm."

On the short drive to Jeff, Sanders, Henry, and Wilson talked excitedly about State's upcoming games with Brandon and A & M.

"We're dreaming," Ed Henry said. "We wouldn't get the bid if the conference *did* end in a tie."

"Sure you would," Soapy said stoutly. "You're the best team around right now. All you have to do is beat Wilson University next Tuesday night."

"They're pretty tough," Sanders mused.

"You'll take 'em," Soapy said. "Chip got fifty-five points against them."

"Fifty-five!" Henry echoed.

"And set a new record," Soapy boasted.

"They went to the semifinals of the Holiday Invitational Tournament, remember," Wilson warned.

"That's the reason you've got to beat them Tuesday night," Soapy concluded. "You beat Wilson University, and we'll take Brandon and A & M. That will mean a green light for you for the NCAA."

"It's a little too much to hope for," Sanders said wistfully.

Chip was listening intently, watching the faces of his Tech friends. *If only Doc Terring will let me play,* he breathed to himself.

The next morning, while Chip was dressing, Soapy read the Sunday papers, commenting as usual on each bit of basketball news. Chip grinned to himself and pre-tended not to notice when the redhead surreptitiously crammed the *News* into the top drawer of his desk.

"Bill Bell says State is cast in the role of a spoiler, Chip. He says we can knock them all out of the running."

"All but Western."

"Southern will take them," Soapy predicted. "Hey, where are *you* going?"

"I'm going to church and then I'm going to take a walk. Then I'm going to study all afternoon."

"Me too. I'll be back after I wash Mitzi's car."

Chip attended church and then walked slowly down Main Street, looking at the store displays, his mind busy with Soapy's problem and the disastrous basketball season. He was startled when someone tapped him on the shoulder. "Thinking about your spring wardrobe?"

Chip pivoted to face Lieutenant Byrnes. "Uh, no," he said, recovering quickly. "I was thinking about Soapy."

Lieutenant Byrnes nodded. "I can understand that. You know, Chip, Fred and Gil would like to help Smith, and in my opinion they will. But you must try to understand their problem. If, as you suggest, the actual thief resembles Smith, Fred and Gil have no other way to strike on the point of resemblance except by talking to Smith and trying to find the key to the mystery."

"Does a red wig sound extreme?"

"Nothing is extreme. Now you take it easy and keep me posted on your progress. We'll get a break on this case before you know it."

"Soapy could stand a break," Chip said.

Byrnes shot a quick glance at him. Then he grasped Chip's shoulder and gave it a little shake. "A man makes his own breaks, Chip. And the real test of a man comes when things look the blackest."

CHAPTER 17

Morale Booster

PETE'S PLACE was deserted. Jimmy Chung was leaning dejectedly on the counter reading the sports pages of
the *News* when Chip came through the front door. Jimmy
quickly closed the paper and tossed it aside. "Hi ya,
Chip," he said ruefully.

"Hey, Jimmy," Chip greeted.

"Well, we just weren't good enough," Jimmy declared,
shaking his head. "If we ever needed you, it was last
night and the night before. Carlton and Riordon both
played possession ball and beat us at our own game."

"How about the press?"

"We tried it. But you're the only real passer we have.
So—"

"I sure wish I could have played."

Jimmy hooked a thumb toward the newspaper. "Did
you read Locke's column today?"

Chip shook his head. "No. I'm not interested. Well, I
just wanted to come see you for a second. I'd better get

back to Jeff and hit the books. See you tomorrow at practice, I hope."

The room was dim and quiet when Chip got back to Jeff. Soapy was still out, so Chip turned on the stereo, sent a few E-mails, and then grabbed a French novel off his shelf and tried to do a little reading. But it was no good. He couldn't get Jimmy's reference to the *News* story out of his mind. Every few pages, Chip's eyes would stray over to Soapy's desk. Eventually, curiosity got the better of him and he looked for the paper. He found it wadded up and crammed in the wastebasket beside Soapy's desk. Soapy had cut Locke's column out of the paper!

Chip tried once more to concentrate on his French. But nothing registered. He shut the book, went to Soapy's desk, and pulled open the drawer. There, on top of a pile of similar clippings, was the one he was seeking: Sunday, February 27. Soapy had neatly printed the date on each article he had cut out of the paper.

Chip started to close the drawer but the urge was too strong. "If it's going to bother me this much," he muttered, "I might as well read it."

STATE OUT OF CONFERENCE RACE

All hopes for the miracle which would keep State in the race for conference honors were dissipated by Carlton and Riordon on Friday and Saturday nights. Carlton played possession basketball Friday night to win, 56-54. Riordon followed the same tact last night to deal the final blow, outlasting State in an uninteresting ball-control game to win, 51-49.

State can now concentrate on Brandon and the "game of the year" against A & M. Although Brandon is still in the running, A & M is a strong favorite for the title and a bid for the NCAA tournament.

While his teammates were battling to stay in the conference race, Chip Hilton, State's scoring star, was resting his knee in preparation for the national marksmanship tournament that will be held in Assembly Hall this coming Friday and Saturday.

WHAT PRICE FOR GLORY?

I looked in vain for a listing of this shooting contest in State's athletic program. Apparently it outranks every team honor in sight (particularly the State University basketball team).

Anger flooded Chip's face as he leafed through the other clippings. Resentment surged through him until he could scarcely control his emotions. Each clipping was equally vicious:

Feb. 25—Hilton remains behind, presumably to practice for the shooting contest.
Feb. 20—State ekes out important win—no thanks to the marksmanship champion.
Feb. 19—Hilton has condescended to play tonight.
Feb. 18—Is Coach Corrigan promoting the AAU Marksmanship Championship Tournament or trying to win games for State? I watched Chip Hilton practice "tourney" shots while his teammates worked on team play.
Feb. 17—How long has Chip Hilton's secret shooting practice been going on? Dr. Mike Terring restricted him from *all* athletics because of his temperamental knee.

That ruined the day for Chip. He went for a long walk and brooded. When he came back, he fought a losing battle with his books. He just couldn't concentrate. Soapy was in a similar state of mind, and the two friends passed a quiet and moody evening.

Chip was nervous when he reported for practice Monday afternoon. But he put on a good show for Murph Kelly and Dr. Terring, and the physician gave him permission to shoot around and limber up his knee. Chip dressed slowly and joined his teammates out on the court. They were low too. But they were glad to see him.

"Sorry we couldn't win, Chip," Barkley said, gripping his hand.

"Sorry I couldn't be there to help," Chip said.

"You helped," Thornhill said, putting his arm over Chip's shoulder. "You carried us through a lot of games. It was about time we did something for you."

"That's right," Gowdy said, joining the circle, "and we're sick and tired of Jim Locke and the way he's been riding you. Just to show him up, we're going to take Brandon and A & M and get Tech an invite to the NCAA if it's the last thing we ever do. Just for you. Right, guys?"

The team's response confirmed everything Kirk and Bradley had said, and Chip couldn't have said anything then to save his life. Fortunately, Coach Corrigan sent him down to the practice basket. *I've got to do my part,* Chip vowed to himself.

Steeling himself to ignore his leg and move freely when he took his shots, Chip forgot all about Jim Locke. Suddenly he felt someone watching him and turned to meet the glance of the one person he least wanted to see.

"How come, Hilton?" Jim Locke asked, grinning. "You too good to practice with the rest of the team?"

Chip's chest contracted. It required an effort to

breathe evenly. "Dr. Terring is the boss," he said slowly. "He said I could only shoot around a little."

"You mean practice for Bill Bell's shooting show, don't you?"

Chip shook his head. "No, Mr. Locke, I don't. I've never intentionally practiced for the marksmanship tournament when I worked out with the team."

Locke eyed Chip warily. "I wonder," he said.

Chip bounced the ball on the floor, counting to himself. When he reached ten, he paused. "That's right, Mr. Locke," he said evenly, twirling the ball in his hands. "I never have."

Chip looked straight into the sportswriter's beady eyes. "But I'll tell you this: I like to shoot, and this week I intend to practice every chance I get. And what's more, I'm going to try my best to retain the shooting championship."

"I can believe that, all right."

Chip bent over and rolled the ball slowly toward Murph Kelly, who was hurrying down the court. Then he straightened up and took a long step toward the columnist. "Now that we understand one another, Mr. Locke," he said, "suppose you leave me alone."

"You can't talk to me like that," Locke cried.

"I think I can," Chip said, advancing toward him.

"Hold it, Chip!" Kelly cried. "Don't do anything foolish." He stepped between the two and faced Locke. "You'd better leave, Mr. Locke. And don't come back until the Coach gives you permission."

Coach Corrigan had approached unheard. "That won't be necessary," he said sharply. "From now on, practices will be closed to everyone." He faced the angry reporter. "And that includes you, Locke. *Particularly* you. Get out!"

Now that was a morale booster! The only event that had done more to build the team's morale than Coach Corrigan's barring Jim Locke from practices was State's victorious conquest of the Holiday Invitational Tournament. The team now came to life with an explosion of energy, and, taking their cue from Chip, the Statesmen's motto became: "Put Tech in the national tournament!"

Chip and Soapy went to the Tech-Wilson game Tuesday night and saw Bill Sanders, Ed Henry, Stew Wilson, and their teammates bring their wonderful season to an end by defeating Wilson, 78-70. Afterward, Chip and Soapy escorted Greg Moran, friend, team captain, and Wilson star scorer, back to Pete's Place.

The victorious Tech team and practically all of the guys from Valley Falls were there celebrating.

"Well, you've done your part," Soapy told the Tech stars. "Now it's up to Chip, Jimmy, and our guys to put you in the tournament. And they're going to do it!"

Soapy was right about defeating Brandon University, but it wasn't easy. When State and Brandon lined up on Wednesday night, the visitors were up and ready for a fight. State was just as eager, but the Statesmen were too tight and tried too hard. Both teams held the ball and played cautiously. The Brandon players used their height and bulk to better advantage under the boards this time and slowly forged ahead.

Coach Corrigan kept Chip out of the game until the last ten minutes. But in those ten minutes, Chip got a lot of practice for the marksmanship tournament. Jimmy, Speed, Sky, and Andy let him do practically all the shooting.

Chip had never felt more confident. He took nine shots and every one of them was for his Tech friends.

Seven of the nine rippled through the cords. Then, with five seconds left to play, he was fouled in the act of shooting and dropped both charity tosses through the hoop to win the game for State, 62-61. And that put Brandon out of the running for the conference championship.

Thursday morning, Soapy was amazed when Chip went downstairs to get the papers and came back up with his nose already in Locke's column in the *News*.

"Listen to this, Soapy," he said, laughing as he marched back in through the door. "Locke says I hogged the ball and took all the team's shots.

"And you know something?" he continued. "He hasn't seen anything yet! I'm going to win the shooting contest, and I'm going to shoot every chance I get against A & M."

Soapy was bewildered. "Are you feeling all right?"

"Sure I'm all right. I'm finally really all right. Now get this! Locke says I'll probably be too exhausted after the Marksmanship Tournament to play in the blood—oh, man, listen to this guy! To play in the 'blood' game against A & M." Chip laughed. "He's sure going to be disappointed, Soapy."

"Of course he is!" Soapy said confidently. "This time Saturday night you'll be the winner and still champion. Now, lemme think. What did I say before? I've got it! Wait and see!"

Just about that time, Bill Bell was concentrating on his column. He stressed the marksmanship tournament, but he didn't forget Tech. He said the Engineers had proved their championship caliber and were entitled to a chance in the NCAA tournament.

Bill Bell grunted with satisfaction as he keyboarded the last word of his article and leaned back in his chair. Then he noticed a copy of the *News* on his desk. He opened it to Jim Locke's column, curious about his rival's thoughts. He read the column several times, frowning and shaking his head angrily. "This is *too* much," he growled.

He sat quietly in his chair for a few seconds and then came to a sudden decision. Back at his computer, he began a letter to Jim Locke. It was a long letter with lots of strong, shoot-from-the-hip advice about the ethical and accurate reporting of news and sports.

Nearly fifty years of experience grounded the philosophy and principles embodied in the contents of that letter. Bell nodded in approval when he signed the final page. "That ought to do it," he murmured, "if Locke possesses any decency at all."

CHAPTER 18

Championship Spot

CHIP WAS embarrassed by all the attention. Photographers surrounded him on all sides, and reporters flung questions at him from all directions. Beyond their faces he could see Soapy, Speed, Biggie, Red, Bill Sanders, Stew Wilson, Ed Henry, Fireball, Whitty, and Jimmy Chung. A little way behind them he saw George Grayson, Mrs. Grayson, and Mitzi Savrill. Mitzi waved her program, and Chip waved back.

"How does it feel to be the two-time champion, Hilton?"

"Were you worried when you missed those two long set shots?"

"Hold it, Hilton. One more please."

"Will you hand him the trophy again, Mr. Coats?"

"That's right, Hilton, reach for it with your left hand and shake hands with the right. Good!"

When all the hoopla was over, Chip's friends broke through, surrounded him, and accompanied him to the locker room. Then they headed to Pete's Place, where the real celebration began. All of Chip's teammates and Coach Corrigan and Henry Rockwell—and even Murph Kelly, who was smiling for a change—were there. The Statesmen and the Valley Falls guys and the Tech stars and Pete Thorpe and the staff from Grayson's were throwing a party in Chip's honor.

It was warm and friendly inside Pete's Place. Outside, it was cold and windy. There were only a few people out on the streets, and they were hurrying along, anxious to gain shelter. But one man was in no hurry. Jim Locke stood at the side of one of the large windows of the restaurant and watched the happy celebration inside. His sharp eyes noted each person, and he paid particular attention to the joy of Chip's basketball teammates, the Statesmen.

Locke stood in the cold a long time, his brow furrowed, a puzzled expression on his face. "I must have had this kid all wrong," he muttered, turning away. "I've made a big mistake. Bill Bell is right." He pulled the hood of his jacket up over his head and walked slowly away, ashamed and buried deep in thought.

It was a real party, with lots of food, good cheer, and basketball talk. Most of it was about Chip's successful defense of his marksmanship title, but some of the talk focused on the upcoming game with A & M and the effect a victory would have on Tech's tournament chances.

Chip was glad to get home when it was all over. The tension had broken with the victory, and now fatigue had set in. He went to bed feeling as if he could stay there for a week. But, strangely, he couldn't sleep. When the first purple ribbon of dawn appeared, he dressed quietly and tiptoed softly out of the room. And when Soapy's alarm rang a half-hour later, Chip was dressed and propped up on his bed reading the papers.

"About time you woke up," Chip teased him. "Here, read Jim Locke's column."

"I thought you were going to stop reading that guy's stuff."

"Coming from you, that's good," Chip said, crossing the room to Soapy's desk. He pulled the drawer open and leafed through the clippings. "Are these yours?"

Soapy pulled the quilt up over his head. "Yeah," he said in muffled tones, "they're mine."

Chip opened the *Herald* to the sports section and read Bill Bell's column.

CHIP HILTON RETAINS HIS
MARKSMANSHIP TITLE

A true champion, Chip Hilton retained his national marksmanship championship last night, marking a first in the history of the tournament.

Chip Hilton has been playing all season for the State varsity basketball team on a bad leg and wanted to withdraw from the tournament many times. But a number of people, including me, prevailed upon him to stick it out.

Unfortunately, there are certain prejudiced people who are obviously unaware of Hilton's contributions to State's University's athletic program—and without the benefit of an athletic scholarship. Hilton, a Dean's List student, is working his way through school and ranks in the top 10 percent of his class.

A picture of the Tech team caught Chip's eye, and he studied the players' faces. Immediately below was a list of their "victims" and the scores. Chip glanced down the basketball score column and then shook Soapy's shoulder. "You can come out now, Soapy. I've got some real news. Southern took Western last night and that puts A & M in the championship spot."

"Temporarily," Soapy growled.

"So," Chip continued, "'Western and Brandon have finished their seasons and are tied for second place with twenty wins and five losses, and A & M leads with a twenty and four record and with one game left to play.'"

"It'll be a three-way tie for first place after Monday," Soapy declared confidently.

"If we win tomorrow night," Chip said jubilantly, "Tech will have a real chance for a berth in the NCAA tournament. A & M, Western, and Brandon won't have enough time to play off the tie. Man, I'm so nervous I can't sit still. I think I'll take a walk."

"In all this rain?"

"Sure. I like to walk in the rain. You better get some more sleep. I'll bring you something to eat when I come back. You and Biggie are on duty tonight. Remember?"

"Yeah, I remember," Soapy said sleepily. "What's my post?"

"You cover the Triangle, and Biggie takes the City watch," Chip said, glancing out the window. "And if it doesn't clear up, it's going to be a tough night."

It was a tough night. The rain had turned to snow when Soapy and Biggie trudged down the front stairs into the cold, miserable night, and Chip felt sorry for them. But he couldn't let anyone fall down on a watch. Every night meant a night closer to catching the robber in action and clearing Soapy's name.

CHAMPIONSHIP SPOT

Chip was just finishing his American literature paper when Biggie showed up at midnight to grab some books and head over to his night internship at State University's physical plant.

"Anything happen?" Chip asked.

Biggie shook his head. "Not a thing. But the store was still open when I left. Well, I'd better get to the plant, Chip. See you in the morning."

Chip proofread and printed out his paper, and then he began to worry. He was determined to stay up until Soapy came home. It was past his training curfew, but ten minutes later he put on his coat and started out for Triangle Mini Mart.

It was only a short hike. Chip chose the most direct route, a service driveway that extended clear across the campus, which was now blanketed by new snow. He strode swiftly along, ignoring his knee. Long before he reached the watch post, he could see that the mini mart's lights were off. Chip debated what to do and then started back to Jeff on one of the wide campus walks, hoping to overtake Soapy.

As he rounded a turn in the walk, he was surprised to see a car blocking the walkway up ahead. A figure was standing near the rear of the car looking helplessly down at a flat tire. The soft, wet snow muffled Chip's steps, and he cleared his throat to give warning of his approach. "Can I give you a hand?" he asked.

The man whirled around quickly, startled and wary. As they stood there appraising each other, Chip tried to catch a glimpse of his face. But that was impossible. The brim of his hat was pulled down over his eyes and the collar of his jacket was turned up around his neck.

"You can't help me," he said gruffly, turning quickly away. "They're both flat. The spare too. Of all the luck!"

He looked up and down the path. "I've got to get one of these tires fixed. In a hurry!"

"The gas stations are probably all closed. I just came from the Triangle—"

He pivoted quickly. "Was it closed?"

"Yes, it was," Chip confirmed.

"I was afraid of that."

"You might try the City. It stays open a little later. It's only seven or eight blocks from here. On the corner of Main and—"

"I know where it is," the guy snapped, turning away. Walking to the back of the car, he yanked the spare out of the trunk and started back along the walk, rolling the tire rapidly through the snow.

Chip walked slowly away, a little irritated by the stranger's attitude. It seemed strange that the guy had driven his car along a campus walkway instead of using one of the regular driveways. The walk was wide enough to be mistaken for a driveway, but this guy appeared to know exactly where he was and where he was going. Why hadn't he used a driveway?

Then, in the distance, Chip heard a police siren and glanced back. The man suddenly froze, then turned and hurried back toward the car, rolling the tire swiftly in front of him.

Suddenly, on a hunch, Chip turned off the path and stepped into the shadow of a tree. He could barely make out the car. Then he heard the engine start and a second later, without lights, the car came bumping along the walk. After the car passed, Chip followed, keeping pace until the car was less than a block away from Jeff.

At the edge of the campus, the driver parked the car in the shadows beside the walk and cut across the lawn to the driveway exit.

Chip could see him peering up and down the street. *He's afraid of being seen,* Chip realized.

He waited, his mind racing from one thought to another. Where was Soapy? A dark car with a light top . . . If only he could get a look at the license plate. "Well," he breathed, "what am I waiting for? He's not going to invite me!"

Chip crept stealthily toward the car, keeping in the shadows, and watching the man intently. Reaching the rear of the car, Chip tried to read the license numbers. But it was too dark. He reached down and tried to feel the raised impressions of the numbers. Then something strange happened. Under the pressure of his fingers, the license plate swung upward and spun until it was in a reversed position. And it remained there!

Chip whistled softly and walked swiftly around the car to try the front plate. It did the same thing and swung upward, revealing only a blank surface. It required a determined tug to pull the plate down.

He glanced toward the driveway again, and at that instant the suspicious man turned and started running back to the car. Chip froze, caught in a moment of panic and indecision.

He waited for a tense split second and then made a sudden decision. Creeping along the side of the car that faced away from the approaching runner, he opened the rear door of the car, praying no interior lights would come on. As he crawled cautiously into the dark car, pressing his body to the floor, his hand encountered a blanket. "What a break," he breathed, pulling the blanket over his elongated form and crowding as far to the other side as possible.

Chip closed the door gently, holding the handle so it wouldn't swing open. "Now I'm in it, and there's no way out," he breathed.

HARDCOURT UPSET

The man's labored breathing was clearly audible now. He slid in behind the wheel and started the engine. The car moved slowly away, swaying slightly as it bumped along on its flat tire. When the driver reached the street, he turned on the headlights. Chip could now see the streetlights and wanted to peer out. But he was afraid to move. He watched the streetlights and figured the driver had covered no more than three blocks before he turned off the main street and proceeded up a rough lane. Now the streetlights grew dim and farther apart.

Chip counted two turns to the right and one to the left. Then, near a dim streetlight, the car slowed, turned left again, and stopped. The driver got out. Chip pulled himself up quietly until he could see over the front seat. The headlights illuminated the man as he glanced furtively around and then hoisted the door of a small garage. He looked about the same age as Chip. Chip lowered himself and held his breath. If he was caught now . . .

Then the man came back and drove the car into the darkness of the garage. Chip waited, scarcely breathing. Now what?

The lights went off, leaving only the dim reflection of the streetlight to illuminate the building. Chip heard the man fumble beneath the front seat before he got out of the car. Chip cautiously raised himself. The guy walked toward the rear of the garage, barely visible in the dim light. Then he paused and took off his hat. After a second, he tossed the hat and a small bundle up on a high shelf and turned around. Chip ducked just in time!

A moment later, the garage door closed gently and Chip heard the click of a lock. The building was in total darkness now. Chip slipped out of the car and moved slowly to a small window at the side of the garage. Next door was a two-story house, stark and lonely but for a gnarled elm tree, its branches swaying in the wind and scraping against an upstairs window.

As he watched, a light flashed on in a window on the second floor. Chip moved away from the window. What to do?

He tried the door, but it wouldn't budge. Objects in the small building began to take shape—a rake, a shovel, a lawn mower—and then the full implications of his position struck Chip. Here he was inside a building trying to get out. This was no joke. He was trespassing on someone's property, and if he forced his way out, he could be accused of breaking and entering. Or, rather, breaking out! Either way, it was still trespassing.

Chip tried to figure out why he had followed his impulse to trail the man. He was thinking about the robberies. But was he justified in going to such extremes? The guy had been jumpy, but that could have been because of the flat tires or because he was late or because of lots of things! The fact that he had been aloof wasn't all that strange. There the guy was, stuck out late at night, and along came a stranger. Maybe he couldn't trust Chip either! And lots of people had dark cars with white tops.

But what about the way the guy ran to the car when he heard the police siren? Well, maybe he hadn't heard the siren. Or he may have figured City Service Station might be closed and made a sudden decision to drive the short distance home on the flat tire. It could have been an old tire. But why did the guy run back to the car from the street? He certainly had acted suspiciously.

"I'm wasting time," he breathed. "I've got to get out of here—in a hurry!"

CHAPTER 19

In the Nick of Time

THE LIGHT from the second-floor window of the house suddenly vanished, and Chip went back over to the garage window. The house was now enveloped in darkness. He tried to find a weakness in the window. He slid his fingers along the top of the frame and found two nails at each corner. They had been driven through the window frame and into the boards on each side. Both sides were firmly nailed closed.

Next Chip tried the door. It was just as strong. He ran his fingers over the door frame, hoping to find a weakness in the wood. But the boards were sturdy. Then he felt the bolts holding the hasp. The small nuts were screwed almost into the wood, and it was impossible to move them.

"If I only had a wrench," he murmured.

He moved cautiously to the back of the building and found a workbench. Several wrenches and other tools were hanging on pegs on the wall, and he found one he thought would fit the nuts on the door's bolts. Working feverishly with the wrench, he finally removed the nuts from the bolts. Then he pushed the door back and forth until he was able to force the bolts out through the holes, and the hasp came free! Now he could open the door.

Chip pushed the door open and inched through the opening. The house was completely dark and there was no one in sight. "What a break!" he whispered, hurrying away. "I'm lucky to get out of this."

Then he thought about Soapy and stopped short. He was getting out, all right, but he hadn't accomplished anything. Not a thing. He could at least get the license plate number.

Doubling back, he slipped back into the garage and picked up the wrench. Working quickly, he removed the front plate and made his way out of the building. He ran the short distance to the streetlight. When he got there, he wrote the name of the street on a piece of paper and quickly copied the numbers from the license plate. Then he returned to the garage, closed the door, and replaced the plate. When Chip emerged from the garage, he didn't know whether he was in luck or in big trouble. But he was going to find out. He had gone too far to back out now.

"I've got to call Lieutenant Byrnes," he told himself. "He'll know what to do."

Chip hurried back to Jeff, his excitement overcoming the stiffness of his knee. "Can't wait to tell Soapy," he whispered, taking the dorm steps two at a time.

But Soapy's bed was empty and still untouched. Chip hesitated long enough to note that the clock showed 2:30. He grabbed the phone.

Lieutenant Byrnes was sleepy and not too enthusiastic until he heard about Chip's adventure. Then his voice became brisk, and his interest sharpened. "You might have something there, Chip," he said sharply, "and in the nick of time too."

"What do you mean, Lieutenant?"

"It's a long story. I'll be at Jeff in ten minutes, and then I'll tell you all about it."

As soon as Chip hung up the phone, he headed for room 216, the last one at the end of the hall and the biggest room on the floor. "Speed, wake up," Chip whispered as he tugged on Morris's shoulders. "Speed, you awake?"

"I am now, man," Speed growled, lifting himself up on his elbows and glancing at the illuminated numbers of his clock radio. "What's wrong? It's the middle of the night!"

"Have you seen Soapy?"

"No, Chip. Isn't he in bed?"

"No, and it doesn't look as if he's been home. He's never done this before. I'm worried."

"Where have *you* been? You're all wet! You're the one who ought to be in bed."

"I know. I'll tell you all about it when I get back. Lieutenant Byrnes is picking me up in a couple of minutes. If you see Soapy, tell him to wait right here with you until I get back."

Speed jumped out of bed and padded down the hall to 212, Chip and Soapy's room. "I'll wait here for him. Hurry back. I want to know what's going on!"

Lieutenant Byrnes pulled up in front of Jeff just as Chip reached the door. On the way to the station, Chip filled him in on all the details.

"I don't know what made me get in the car, Lieutenant."

"It wasn't very smart, Chip," the officer spoke firmly. "You might have gotten into serious trouble. Especially if he *is* the man we're after."

"Is there any way we can find out?"

"Perhaps. We'll follow up on it. First, we've got to see Parks and Minton. Now, Chip, brace yourself. I've got some bad news for you."

"Soapy?"

"That's right. The Triangle was held up again. A little after midnight."

"But Soapy was on watch, right there!"

"Parks and Minton figure differently. They arrived less than a minute after Welsh was robbed, and they picked Smith up a couple of minutes later. And he was running. Running away at full speed."

Detective Fred Parks was annoyed. He strode back and forth in front of Soapy, shooting one question after another at the unhappy redhead. Gil Minton was sitting behind the table studying his notebook, and Welsh was squirming around uneasily on a chair opposite Soapy.

"I don't have any money," Soapy said firmly, "and I never had a gun, and I didn't have anything to do with the holdup. When I saw Welsh turn out the lights, I started for the hot-dog stand to get a sandwich."

"Why were you running?"

Soapy sighed deeply and shook his head. "*I told you.* I run every day. I like to keep in shape."

The questioning was at a stalemate when Lieutenant Byrnes and Chip arrived.

Chip had seen Soapy in a lot of tough situations during their many years of friendship, but he had never seen the redhead in such a sorry state. Soapy's face was scarlet, and his freckles stood out in small blotches. He looked like he had the measles. Although the temperature in the room was a little on the cold side, perspiration ringed his forehead and slid in trails down his cheeks. But he was full of fight.

"What's he doing here?" Parks asked, jerking his head toward Chip.

"I think he's got some information that may interest you," Byrnes replied softly.

"Oh, no!" Parks groaned. "Please—"

"He's got something that looks hot to me. You tell him, Chip."

Chip told the detectives about the car, the lack of headlights, the flat tire, its location on a campus walkway instead of a driveway, the license plates, and the man's strange actions when he heard the police siren. "And it was a dark car with a light top," he concluded, waiting expectantly.

"There was no car tonight," Parks said sharply. "The man was on foot."

"But couldn't he have left his car on campus and walked to the Triangle?"

"That he could," Parks admitted. "However, you're overlooking an important point. We saw Smith running away from the station."

"What about the money?" Soapy demanded. "Welsh says the man took over two hundred dollars. If I had robbed him and was running away from the place, wouldn't I have the money?"

"You could have dropped it," Minton interrupted. "I—"

"Hold it, Gil," Byrnes said hastily. "I don't want to break in on your case, but a lot of things in Hilton's story add up."

"What do you want us to do?" Minton asked. "We can't wake a man up in the middle of the night and ask him if he's a robber just because Hilton says he was acting suspiciously."

"That's right," Parks added. "We can check the license number and try to get a warrant in the morning."

Byrnes nodded. "I know. But that might be too late."

"Excuse me," Chip said. "Couldn't you take Mr. Welsh out there to look at the car?"

"Yes, but why?" Parks said.

"Well," Chip continued, "if it's the same kind of a car the robber used in the other holdups, couldn't you wake up the man and tell him about what I did to his garage door?"

"And then?" Parks prompted.

"Then, if Mr. Welsh recognizes the man, couldn't you arrest him? Or at least bring him in for questioning—like you do with Soapy?"

"I imagine we could," Parks said dryly. A brief smile flashed across his lips. "But you seem to have forgotten that Welsh has already identified Smith."

"But it hasn't been very convincing," Chip persisted.

Parks looked at Minton and waved his hands helplessly. "What do you say, Gil?"

"It's worth a try. We're not making much progress with Smith. What will we do with *him?*"

"Take him along," Byrnes said quickly.

Soapy gulped and looked at Chip. "Am I glad to see you! I'm beginning to think Speed's right. We oughta call his father. The way this thing is going, it looks like I might need a lawyer, Chip."

"If things don't get cleared up now, I'll call Mr. Morris first thing in the morning, Soapy."

Lieutenant Byrnes and Chip led the way and Detective Minton drove his car with Soapy, Welsh, and Parks. Lieutenant Byrnes drove directly to the street and parked at the corner. Then the group proceeded on foot to the garage. Inside, Minton and Parks focused their flashlights on the car and turned to Welsh.

"Yep, it looks like the car, all right," said the mini mart employee.

"So far so good," Byrnes said.

"Maybe," Parks muttered. "Check the plates, Gil."

Detective Minton examined the rear plate, lifting it just as Chip had done. Then he moved to the front of the car and tried the front plate. "Nothing much wrong, Fred," he said a moment later. "The plates have long bolts holding them to the frame and they do spin, but that doesn't mean much."

"All right," Parks said impatiently, "come along. We'll soon know."

When they reached the porch, Parks waved them away from the door. "*I'll* do the talking."

Chip moved close to Soapy and elbowed him sharply. "This is it, Soapy!"

"Quiet!" Minton hissed. "Move back." They grouped in the shadows while Parks pressed the doorbell several times. Moments later, a hall light flashed on, and a man peered out through the curtained window of the door. Then he turned on the porch light and, seeing Minton's extended badge, opened the door. "What is it?" he asked sharply. "What do you want?"

"We're police officers," Parks said shortly. "Can we talk to you?"

The man hesitated momentarily, cautiously eyeing Detective Parks and his companions. "Sure," he said reluctantly. "Step inside."

They filed into the small hallway and followed the man into the living room.

"Is this the man, Welsh?" Parks asked. Welsh scrutinized the man carefully and shook his head. "I never saw him before in my life," he said confidently. "It's not the man. He's too old."

"Well, that's that!" Parks said.

IN THE NICK OF TIME

"Just a second," Chip interrupted. "This man is too tall and, excuse me, sir, but like Mr. Welsh said, he's too old. The man driving the car was no taller than Soapy and around our age. He was built just like Soapy."

Parks held out his hand to silence Chip. "Just a second." He turned to the man. "Is that your car—the one in the garage next door?"

"No. It belongs to a kid who rooms with us, Justin Williams."

"Is he here?"

"If the car is in the garage, he's here. He's probably asleep. Do you want me to wake him up?"

Parks nodded. "Yes, I do. I'll go with you, if you don't mind. Gil, suppose you come along. The rest of you wait here."

Chip, Soapy, Lieutenant Byrnes, and Welsh waited impatiently as the officers and the house owner ascended the steps. After a short silence there was a knock on a door. A muffled conversation followed. Chip was counting the seconds, his shoulder braced firmly against Soapy. Then they heard footsteps coming down the stairs, and a well-built young man, dressed in sweats, appeared in the doorway of the living room. Parks and Minton pressed closely behind him.

Welsh leaped to his feet and pushed forward. "It looks like him," he said, puzzlement registering in his voice. "But he ain't got red hair!"

"What's this all about?" the young man demanded aggressively. "What are you wakin' me up in the middle of the night for?"

"I'm sorry, sir," Parks appeased. "We made a mistake."

They trooped down the porch steps and started back toward the cars parked at the corner. Behind them, the door slammed shut, and the porch light went out.

"Hilton," Parks said icily, "I hope you'll stick to your school books and games and let us handle the police department."

"What about the garage?" Minton asked. "We didn't tell him—"

"That's right!" Chip cried excitedly. "The garage! I forgot something. Wait! I'll be right back."

CHAPTER 20

The Fabulous Five

CHIP TURNED and dashed back up the street and through the open door of the garage. He edged through the darkness beside the car until he reached the rear of the building. Reaching up, he felt along the shelf and pulled down the bundle the driver had stashed there. Even in the dark Chip could tell he was clutching a hat. Inside was a hairy object.

"A wig!" he cried exultantly, dashing out of the garage. At the corner, he extended the hat toward Detective Parks. "It's a brown hat, and here's a wig and a clear plastic mask!"

Welsh grabbed the wig out of Chip's hand. "Yahoo!" he gurgled excitedly. "And it's red! Lemme see that hat! This is it. There's the two feathers! Just like I said. It's him! It's him!"

"Could be, all right," Minton agreed.

Detective Parks nodded. "Yes, it sure could. We'd better ask our new friend a few more questions."

They made their way back to the porch. The owner appeared almost as soon as the detective touched the bell. "Now what?" he demanded.

"We need to talk to your renter again."

The man gestured up the steps. "You know where his room is."

He watched Parks and Minton take the steps two at a time and turned to Lieutenant Byrnes. "Don't you cops need some kind of a warrant to bust into a man's house like this?"

"But we didn't bust in, sir," Lieutenant Byrnes said evenly. "You let us in."

"Sure. It was let you in or else—"

"Oh, I don't think it was that bad."

They were interrupted by descending steps, and through the open door Chip saw Justin Williams, the guy built just like Soapy, sandwiched between the two detectives.

"In here," Minton said, hooking a thumb toward the living room. They filed into the room, and Lieutenant Byrnes motioned to Chip, Soapy, and Welsh to follow. Then the familiar questioning began. It was the usual procedure, with Detective Parks shooting the questions one after another and Minton taking down the answers in his notebook.

"What's your name?"

"Justin Williams. Why?"

"Is this your hat?"

"Sure. It looks like my hat."

Parks held up the red wig. "This yours too?"

"Yeah. So what?"

"Is that your car in the garage?"

"Yeah."

"Did you use it tonight?"

"Sure. I use it every night."

"Why?"

Williams shrugged his shoulders and repeated the question. "Why? To get home. I'm on the four-to-eleven shift out at Martin's."

"So you got off work at eleven o'clock. Then what did you do?"

"I came straight home."

Parks dangled the wig in the air. "What do you use this for?"

"Oh, just for fun. Masquerades and things."

"Recognize anyone in this room?"

Williams looked blankly at the ring of faces and shook his head. "No, I don't know any of them."

Chip started to protest, but Welsh beat him to it. "It's the same voice!" he said. "Make him put on the wig and the mask and the hat."

Williams whirled and sprinted toward the door.

But he wasn't fast enough. Gil Minton grabbed his arm and pulled him back. "Wait a second there."

Minton pushed the suspect into a chair and turned to Parks. "Now what?"

"I think I'll have a little look at the room upstairs," Parks said, turning to the house owner. "Mind going along?"

Everybody waited quietly. All except Welsh. He put on a real show. "I knew you all the time, Williams," he exulted, nodding his head vigorously. "You couldn't fool me. I was just waiting for you to make a false move."

"Yeah, right!" Soapy exclaimed. "But you've forgotten something."

"What?"

"The blue sweater, remember?"

Welsh nodded soberly. "That's right. Maybe he's not the man after all. But I'll know when I see him all dressed up. Brown hat, red wig, white face, blue sweater, and clear mask. I guess I'd better tell those two detectives to look for that blue sweater."

"We won't need the sweater," Detective Parks said, coming rapidly down the stairs. "I think we've got about all the evidence we need."

"What kind of evidence?" Welsh demanded.

"Money!" Parks said. "Lots of it." He turned to Soapy. "Well, Smith, this lets you off the hook. You're no longer under suspicion."

"Oh, man!" Soapy said, grinning with his usual spontaneity. "I'm off the hook before I'm booked!"

"But it was close," Gil Minton reminded him, putting his arm around Soapy's shoulders. "You're lucky to have such a persistent friend."

"You sure are," Parks added. "Are you sure you're not majoring in criminal justice up at that college, Hilton?"

"Positive," Chip said, sighing with relief. "No more cops-and-robbers for me."

Minton laughed. "Good!" He turned to Soapy. "I know you'll find this hard to believe, Smith, but Fred and I felt sure all along that you were innocent."

"Even if we did give you a rough time," Parks said, grinning.

"It was rough all right," Soapy agreed ruefully. Then the mischief was back in his eyes. "Say, Mr. Parks, did you ever study history? Ever study the Inquisitors?"

Parks shook his head. "The *Inquisitors?* Never heard of them. Who were they?"

"Oh, just a bunch of people who lived five hundred years or so ago. You sure you never read about them?"

Parks grinned. "Maybe I ought to go back to school and study up on these—er—*Inquisitors.*"

"Please don't!" Soapy said quickly, grimacing. "You

know more about inquisitioning than they ever dreamed."

"Well," Parks said dryly, "if you're sure I couldn't learn anything—"

"I'm sure," Soapy said grimly. "You wrote the book!"

It was four o'clock when they got back to the police station. Justin Williams was booked immediately, and then Chip and Welsh signed statements for the record. While this was going on, Lieutenant Byrnes was on the phone calling the *News* and *Herald*. Soapy listened in, a big smile spreading over his face from ear to ear.

When Chip and Soapy reached Jeff, it was nearly daylight on the morning of the biggest game of the year, the game against State's bitter rivals, A & M. And Chip Hilton had broken curfew.

"Chip," Soapy fretted, "if Coach Corrigan finds out you were up all night, he'll throw the book at you. Maybe even throw you off the team."

"He won't have to *find* out," Chip said wearily. "I'll tell him myself. Tonight. Just before the game."

"You think you should play tonight?"

Chip nodded. "I'll play if he puts me in. It's up to the coach."

"Boy, will the guys be surprised when they hear about the holdup!" Soapy exclaimed. "You know something? I'm not going to tell a soul. I just want to see their faces when they read about it in the papers."

"It won't be in the *News*. It's too late to meet the deadline."

"Forget the *News*," Soapy said, wrinkling up his nose. "Just so it's in the *Herald*."

"How are you going to keep all this secret until the paper comes out?"

"I'll keep it. You won't tell, will you?"

Chip yawned and shook his head. "Don't worry about me. I've only got one class this morning. Then I'm heading back to the dorm for some sleep. I'll probably sleep until it's time for the game."

Meanwhile, the papers got the story, and as soon as Chip Hilton's name was mentioned, the night desks at the *News* and the *Herald* called their respective sports editors, Jim Locke and Bill Bell, who listened avidly to the details.

Chip didn't show up when his friends gathered at the Student Union for lunch. "See the *News?*" Biggie asked.

"Sure did!" Soapy said quickly. "Wait until Chip sees this!"

"Imagine Dr. Terring writing to Locke," Speed said.

Biggie nodded. "And imagine Locke printing the letter!"

"Listen!" Soapy said, pulling a clipping out of his pocket. "I'll read it. 'Dear Mr. Locke.'"

"Why don't you read Locke's preliminary paragraph?" Biggie asked.

"Good idea," Soapy said, starting again. "Listen! 'This reporter is printing two letters that were received some time ago. They speak for themselves.' Now comes the letter."

Dear Mr. Locke,

As team physician for State University, it is my duty to advise you that Chip Hilton has been under my personal care since he was injured in the Christmas basketball tournament in Springfield. Driven by his great loyalty to State and to his teammates, Hilton has played despite his injury and has suffered intense physical pain every time he participated in a game.

Time and again, it has been necessary for me to order him to the sidelines, despite his persistent pleas that he be permitted to play. His devotion to the team and to the game of basketball has won the admiration of his fellow players, his coaches, and his team physician.

> Sincerely yours,
> Mike Terring, M.D.

Soapy was beaming. "How about that?"

"How about this?" Fireball chimed in, poking his finger into the paper where the next letter was. "'Hilton's devotion to the university and the team has been an inspiration to all of us who were aware of his desire to help us win.'"

Fireball held the clipping up so the rest could see. "Look! That's signed by every player on the team. Look at their names: Barkley, Thornhill, Gowdy, Reardon, Bollinger, Jimmy, Speed, of course, J. C. Tucker, and all the rest! That was a great thing to do for Chip!"

"Wait until Chip sees Locke's column," Whitty said. "He won't believe it!"

"Forget about Locke," Soapy said. "Wait until you see the *Herald* this afternoon!"

"What about the *Herald?*" Speed demanded.

"Oh, nothing," Soapy said mysteriously.

"You holding something out on us?" Fireball growled.

"Maybe," Soapy said gleefully. "Well, I've got to go to work. See you all at the game tonight."

Two hours later, practically everyone in University was reading the *Herald,* and the reason for Soapy's exuberance was obvious.

The issue of the *Herald* should have been called the "Chip Hilton Edition." Chip's picture was on the front page with a complete story of his part in the capture of the "midnight phantom." And he was mentioned in practically every column of the sports section.

The front-page story caused a lot of talk around University, but the stories on the sports pages drew the most attention. At Grayson's, Soapy, Mitzi, Fireball, Whitty, and Mr. Grayson all bought copies. They were sitting on the couches enjoying the stories together.

"Bill Bell says State and Chip Hilton can put Tech in the NCAA tournament tonight," Fireball said elatedly. "Listen! 'If State can topple A & M tonight, the conference race will be thrown into a three-way tie between A & M, Western, and Brandon, each with twenty victories and five defeats. Looking beyond this big *if,* I talked this morning with Dan Wright, chairman of the NCAA tournament selection committee, and he suggested that if State defeats A & M tonight, Tech would undoubtedly rank as one of the hottest contenders for an invitation.'"

"I like this part best of all," George Grayson said, reading aloud from the paper: "'State's entire student body will be pulling for a victory over A & M tonight so State's local sports' rivals have a shot at the tournament.'"

"Isn't that great?" Whitty said happily.

And listen to this, Grayson read, stressing the words, "'*Every* starter on Tech's fabulous five is on the Dean's List and—' Hey! Hold it! We're getting jammed up. We've got work to do, people!"

"Don't forget to stop at Pete's for something for Chip to eat," Fireball reminded Soapy as he and Whitty went back behind the old-fashioned soda fountain to fill some orders.

"You can use my car, Soapy," Mitzi added, her eyes flashing. "But let's not have any more flat tires."

"Never again," Soapy said solemnly, rolling his eyes. "Never, never again!"

Chip was just getting up when Soapy arrived with the papers and a complete chicken dinner, compliments of Pete Thorpe and Jimmy Chung. The redhead could barely conceal his excitement.

"Read the papers," he said. "Read the *News* first."

"I'll eat first," Chip said, enjoying Soapy's impatience. When he finished his last bite of coleslaw, Chip leisurely read the papers and dressed without making any comment. Soapy didn't get it.

"What's the matter, Chip? I thought you'd get a real charge out of it."

"I did."

"But you haven't said a word."

"Do I *have* to say something, Soapy? I think it's great. But right now I'm thinking only about the game tonight. It means everything."

Coaches Jim Corrigan and Henry Rockwell were in the basketball office when Chip arrived at Assembly Hall. Corrigan saw him pass the door and charged after him. "Hey, Chip!" he cried. "Come here! We were just talking about you. I guess everybody's talking about you. How's your knee?"

"It's fine, Coach. I'd like to tell you about last night—"

"Forget about last night!" Corrigan interrupted. "You report to Murph and let Dr. Terring look at that knee."

Henry Rockwell slapped Chip on the back. "Right. That little infraction last night might just turn out to be the best break of the year."

"Especially for Soapy," Corrigan added.

"Then you know about—"

"About Soapy?" Corrigan interrupted. "Sure, Chip. Detective Byrnes is one of my best friends. Rock and I have been in on that little difficulty almost from the beginning. We were keeping our eye on the situation. But that can wait. Right now you better report to Murph. He's waiting for you."

As soon as Chip pushed open the locker room door, he was mobbed by his teammates. They circled him and roughed him up with enthusiastic affection.

"It's old Sherlock Holmes himself!"

"Where's your cap and pipe?"

"Man, you know he doesn't smoke!"

"What did you think about Locke's article?"

"See our names? See what we said?"

"Tonight's the night, Chipper. This is the night we put Tech in the tournament. For you!"

Murph Kelly came pushing through the mob of players. "Come on, come on," he said roughly. "Chip's due for a little visit with Doc Terring."

Kelly hustled Chip away from his teammates. "This may be the last game of the season, Chip, but it's not going to be *your* last game. Not if I can help it. Come on. We're going to see Terring."

Terring examined Chip's knee thoroughly and carefully tested the ligament with his fingertips as Murph Kelly flexed and then extended the leg. "It's coming along, Murph," he said gently. "Two or three weeks' rest, and it will be as good as new."

"The game tonight means a lot to me, Doc," Chip said simply. "I'd like to help win it."

"I know, Chip. I'll talk to Coach Corrigan. We'll leave it this way. If you're needed badly toward the end of the game, I'll tell Coach he can use you. But only for a couple of minutes." He glanced at Kelly and nodded significantly. "That's it, Murph."

CHAPTER 21

History Can Repeat

ASSEMBLY HALL was jammed that night. The parking lot was packed well before 6:00 P.M. for the 7:00 tip-off, and latecomers scrambled for parking spots as far downtown as the city square. A sea of crimson and blue moved like waves rushing to a shore as State University fans took their seats, filling the stadium with a capacity crowd of fifteen thousand in anticipation of the season finale.

The band's bass drums reverberated to the ceiling as State University's male cheerleaders zipped up and down the court, waving huge State University banners, and girls dressed in red and blue skirts jumped and leaped and flipped across the gleaming hardcourt. ESPN cameras were prepared to capture the TV action, and the scorers' table was already set with an electronic feast as announcers put on their headsets and sportswriters positioned themselves behind their laptops.

And down the long corridor, Chip could feel the tension in the locker room. His teammates felt it too. It was something they couldn't explain, something they could only feel.

When the Statesmen walked down that long hallway and first broke onto the court, there was a brief silence, and then the tension exploded as the crowd hailed them with a flood of cheers. Chip came last, trying but finding it difficult to conceal his limp. Then the cheers became a thundering roar as the fans rose en masse to tell Chip Hilton how they felt about him.

The cheers came rolling down around Chip, Soapy, Corrigan, Rockwell, Murph, Doc Terring, and all of the Statesmen just as they had at Springfield when State had cinched the Holiday Invitational Tournament.

And at the scorers' table, Bill Bell was on his feet applauding just as if he were a State University student and one of Chip Hilton's biggest fans. Then Bell got one of the biggest shocks of his life. Someone tapped him on the shoulder. Bell turned and his eyes widened in shocked surprise. It was Jim Locke.

But not the Jim Locke Bill Bell knew. This man was almost a stranger. Locke's habitual sneer was gone, replaced by a quiet sincerity. His eyes were level and steady, and he extended his hand with a gesture of humility. Then, despite the surprised stares of his colleagues—the other sportswriters—Locke moved forward beside Bell and joined in the applause.

Then the game was underway. Bill Bell turned to say something to Locke. But what Bell saw in the rival sportswriter's eyes made him change his mind; he said what he had to say with a smile and a clasp of Locke's hand. Words wouldn't have meant anything then anyway. Sometimes there is a quality of action, of presence, that compels us more than words.

The tumult continued unabated all through the

game. A & M played brilliantly and won a share of the crowd's acclaim, but the fans were there to cheer the Statesmen to victory. And they weren't going to settle for anything less. And time after time, a cheer came rolling down. "Put Tech in the tournament! Put Tech in the tournament!" It was punctuated by other cheers calling for Chip: "We want Hilton! We want Hilton!"

But Coach Corrigan was following Mike Terring's orders, and Chip stayed on the bench. At the half, A & M led, 45-41. And the Aggies were still out in front after ten minutes into the second half, 62-58. Coach Corrigan still made no move to put Chip in the game, despite the pleas and chants of the fans.

With less than three minutes left to play in the game, State battled back to tie the score, 79-79. Then the great Aggies pivot star, Lloyd Jenkins, scored on a jump shot to put A & M in the lead, 81-79. Barkley's closed hand raised over his head indicated State was calling for a time-out.

The fans recognized the opportunity, stamping their feet and chanting in unison: "We want Hilton! We want Hilton!"

Chip leaned forward on the bench, every fiber of his being tensed and poised and waiting for Corrigan's nod. "Now," he breathed. "It's got to be now."

But Corrigan passed him up, shook his head decisively, and beckoned to Gowdy. Then the fans really went berserk. Assembly Hall became a bedlam of deafening, ear-shattering chaos. Cheerleaders somersaulted across the floor, their red-and-blue skirts fluttering with the force, while others were propelled into the air and caught by their male counterparts, and all the while the band played State's fight song with enough energy to make the very walls of the building vibrate.

HARDCOURT UPSET

Time was in now, and the Statesmen were desperate,— their big game was slipping away. They tightened up, failed to drive, and handled the ball as if they were from another planet. The A & M players sensed State's indecisive, tentative play and pressed forward, forcing their rivals back toward the ten-second line. Then Barkley called another time-out, and Coach Corrigan turned toward the bench.

Chip was poised and waiting and on his feet as soon as Coach Corrigan turned. But fast as he was, the reaction of the crowd was faster. Their shouts of approval became one continuous roar. Coach Corrigan was talking excitedly in the huddle, but Chip didn't hear a thing he said.

Then he was out on the floor, moving on two wobbly legs that he feared he couldn't control. But Jimmy Chung took care of that. He hit him with a pass and cut in front of Chip's guard, setting up a perfect screen. Chip's confidence returned. He concentrated on the hoop and took the shot. The ball went up and out in a perfect arc, swishing neatly through the net.

The score was tied now, 81-81, with less than a minute left to play. The Aggies took the ball out of bounds under their basket, and State hawked them all over the court. But the Statesmen were fearful of fouling, and the Aggies had little trouble advancing past the ten-second line.

Chip could hear Soapy, Bill Sanders, Ed Henry, and Stew Wilson yelling. "Come on, Chip! Come on, Chip! Get the ball! Get the ball!"

And then, strangely and suddenly, Chip felt he had been through all this before.

"History *can* repeat itself," he breathed. "It's got to!"

Except for the uniforms, the faces, and the score, the

situation was the same as it had been at Springfield in the final seconds of the championship game. Then, too, the score had been tied. And the great Southwestern team had held the ball then, had played for one shot, just as A & M was doing now.

Chip glanced at Jimmy and then at the clock. Jimmy had made the interception in the Southwestern game.

But A & M was playing it safe; the Aggies held the ball and watched the clock. And they kept the court open and were wary, faking before every pass. Again Chip glanced at Jimmy. "It's up to you, Jimmy," he whispered. "Come on! Get the ball!"

Bouncing from the rafters and from the walls, and rolling down and around the players on the floor, came the giant echo of the crowd: "Get the ball! Get the ball!"

Jimmy didn't seem to hear a thing. He never looked at the ball, concentrating solely on his man and playing a tight man-to-man defense instead.

Chip glanced at the clock. Twenty seconds to play! Now A & M began to move, maneuvering for the last shot. The shot which could mean the conference championship, the bid to the nationals.

Fifteen seconds . . . fourteen . . . thirteen . . . twelve . . . eleven . . . ten . . . nine . . .

Then it happened! Just as it had happened before. Just as Chip knew it would happen again, time and time again, in this great game of uncertainties, in this great game of basketball.

Jimmy shot forward like a flash of light. He seemed to move even more swiftly than the ball and made a lightning-fast stab at the leather as it flew toward Jenkins under the basket. It was a desperate thrust, a last-gasp try for the ball. Jimmy nearly did it! But not quite. His straining fingers deflected the flying sphere, but not enough for control. The ball went spinning across the court. It was anybody's ball!

Every player on the floor, it seemed, dove for the ball. But it was Sky Bollinger who reached it first. Sky took off in a flying dive, and his long arm swept the ball away from the scrambling mob. The ball was nearly out of bounds when Chip caught it up and cast a frantic glance at the clock. Four seconds!

Then Chip saw the flying form of Jimmy Chung. Jimmy had kept on going. He was speeding far down the court. All alone!

Chip's reaction was automatic; a replica of many a lightning pass on the football field. He threw the ball straight for the basket, giving Jimmy the same kind of lead he would have given a speeding end.

The ball and Jimmy converged on the basket, and the speeding little ball handler barely made it. He sprang high in the air and stabbed at the ball. A split second after his fingers twisted the ball and let go, the game horn drilled through the roar of the crowd. Then, just as if someone had pulled a giant switch, the crowd roar ceased.

Chip pulled his body far to the left, trying to impart direction to the ball from all that distance. He saw that the spinning sphere was impossibly out of line for a perfect arc into the hoop. He groaned and started for the bench. "Overtime," he muttered, "overtime."

Then the ball kissed the glass backboard in the upper right-hand corner and went spinning, almost miraculously, to the left. Chip thought his eyes had tricked him. He stared as the ball darted away from the transparent glass and went spinning through the hoop and into the net.

The ball hesitated just a fraction of a second, taking

a little swing in the net, as if to tease the spectators, before it swished on through and dropped to the floor.

Then, from nowhere, right up out of the floor it seemed to Chip, his teammates and the fans were around him and lifting him to their shoulders. Chip twisted around and saw that Jimmy was caught up by another cheering throng of fans. Jimmy was yelling at him, his triumphant fist raised in the air. Memories of Springfield and the Holiday Invitational Tournament rushed into his mind—he and Jimmy had been hoisted above the crowd then, just as they were now.

Chip was almost deafened by the tremendous roar of the happy State fans as they yelled and cheered and applauded and tugged at him. But in spite of the turmoil, he heard Soapy and Bill Sanders and Ed Henry and Stew Wilson.

"Chip! You did it! You did it!"

And from atop those shoulders, Chip Hilton searched frantically through the crowd in the stands until he caught and held the eyes he was looking for. And from atop those shoulders and from high up in the stands, it seemed as if everything was moving in slow motion, somehow carrying them both back and across time to Valley Falls. Snapshot images of two little boys playing catch in the shelter and the protection of the Hilton's backyard "Athletic Club"—a perfect battery—blended into days upon days at Valley Falls High School under the guidance of the Rock and then fast forwarded to the present, to the here and now, where two young men were learning to stand on their own, to face adversity and to claim victory for themselves and others.

And just as Soapy had been there for him all those times, from his dad's death to his mom's illness, through triumph and through disappointments, so had Chip been there for Soapy. Yes, it seemed Soapy's presence had always been there, and now Chip had been there for him, shoulder to shoulder. Soapy, the seemingly irrepressible, Soapy the giver, Soapy Smith, the true friend.

And with enhanced wisdom, in one of those rare moments of complete communication, a communion of the spirit that requires no words, they knew they would always be friends—they would always be there for each other. And their eyes held and never flickered.

And in that moment Soapy came to understand what Chip had meant—some things don't have to be said because you just know them. And in that boisterous, cheering, celebrating crowd, Chip and Soapy, with a quiet assurance, both knew—just as they would always know and would always be there for each other.

Afterword

AS WE USHER in the new millennium, as historians and scholars record the phenomenal growth of the twentieth century, as well as reflect on the many changes of this era, the core values we hold as constant remain the foundation of our country and society.

We have seen many changes in the sport of basketball in this century. The recent ones reflect the times we live in—the explosion of the sport on television, the *size and speed* of the players that play the game, the unprecedented worldwide exposure, and the influence of money. But the core of the game, what it teaches, its values, and how we benefit from it stays the same. Basketball provides unlimited pleasure to many. It teaches the true meaning of the human spirit, the understanding of character, as well as providing many comparisons between the sport and the influences it has on our everyday life. Nowhere are these values and ideas more exemplified or articulated than in the *Chip Hilton Sports* series of books that reflect the philosophy and human quality of Hall of Fame Coach Clair Bee.

I am honored to be asked to add a few thoughts to this great series and attempt to reduce the many years of wonderful experiences I've had in the game of basketball into a clear message or statement.

Through all the years, the many games, the young men that I've had the privilege to coach, the opportunities the game has afforded me, I'm humbled to be linked with the name Clair Bee. And as I reflect on the legacy of this man and the stories and examples presented in the Chip Hilton series, I'm struck by one thought that I believe I share with Coach Bee.

When the whistles have gone silent, the games are over, and the young men or boys we've worked with are grown, our greatest reward is when we see them not as players but as adults and when we hear from them about their life experiences and the impact we have had on them as coaches and men. An example of such a feeling is captured in a letter I recently received from a former player.

> *"Make sure to reiterate to your players how truly special playing college basketball is. You always told us about appreciating every experience you have while in college. It really goes by fast and like most good things you do not realize how good it is until it is gone. There is something truly special about a college basketball team. You have black, white, rich, poor, all coming together to play a game of basketball. You share a common goal and support each other to get there, because deep down inside you know you need all*

*your teammates, whatever their role. It is
more than just wins and losses. It is all
the blood, sweat, and tears that go into a
season from the first day of conditioning
to the final buzzer of the last game. There
is nothing like sharing celebration over a
big victory. Even more special is the way
a team comes together in a time of loss,
seeing a locker room full of young men
crying over a defeat is not just a sign of
sadness but a sign of togetherness. There
is the sacred institution called the "locker
room" where men are made and brother-
hood prevails. I fondly miss it all."*

This young man was not a star as a player but, like
many, contributed in countless ways for the betterment
of the team. He has made a lasting impression on me and
confirmed my feelings of privilege and honor at being a
basketball coach.

Clair Bee has had an enormous effect on so many
people, through his coaching, teaching, and writings, and
to be able to share my thoughts on the game of basketball through this book has been a true gift.

JIM O'BRIEN
Men's Basketball Coach
The Ohio State University

Your Score Card

I have   I expect
read: to read:

_____ _____ 1. **Touchdown Pass:** The first story in the series, introducing you to William "Chip" Hilton and all his friends at Valley Falls High during an exciting football season.

_____ _____ 2. **Championship Ball:** With a broken ankle and an unquenchable spirit, Chip wins the state basketball championship and an even greater victory over himself.

_____ _____ 3. **Strike Three!** In the hour of his team's greatest need, Chip Hilton takes to the mound and puts the Big Reds in line for all-state honors.

_____ _____ 4. **Clutch Hitter!** Chip's summer job at Mansfield Steel Company gives him a chance to play baseball on the famous Steeler team where he uses his head as well as his war club.

_____ _____ 5. **A Pass and a Prayer:** Chip's last football season is a real challenge as conditions for the Big Reds deteriorate. Somehow he must keep the team together for their coach.

_____ _____ 6. **Hoop Crazy:** When three-point fever spreads to the Valley Falls basketball varsity, Chip Hilton has to do something, and fast!

YOUR SCORE CARD

I have I expect
read: to read:

____   ____   7. *Pitchers' Duel:* Valley Falls participates in the state baseball tournament, and Chip Hilton pitches in a nineteen-inning struggle fans will long remember. The Big Reds year-end banquet isn't to be missed!

____   ____   8. *Dugout Jinx:* Chip is graduated and has one more high school game before beginning a summer internship with a minor-league team during its battle for the league pennant.

____   ____   9. *Freshman Quarterback:* Early autumn finds Chip Hilton and four of his Valley Falls friends at Camp Sundown, the temporary site of State University's freshman and varsity football teams. Join them in Jefferson Hall to share successes, disappointments, and pranks.

____   ____   10. *Backboard Fever:* It's nonstop basketball excitement! Chip and Mary Hilton face a personal crisis. The Bollingers discover what it means to be a family, but not until tragedy strikes their two sons.

____   ____   11. *Fence Busters:* Can the famous freshman baseball team live up to the sportswriter's nickname or will it fold? Will big egos and an injury to Chip Hilton divide the team? Can a beanball straighten out an errant player?

____   ____   12. *Ten Seconds to Play!* When Chip Hilton accepts a job as a counselor at Camp All-America, the last thing he expects to run into is a football problem. The appearance of a junior receiver at State University causes Coach Curly Ralston a surprise football problem too.

HARDCOURT UPSET

I have   I expect
read: to read:

____   ____   13. *Fourth Down Showdown:* Should Chip Hilton and his fellow sophomore stars be suspended from the State University football team by Coach Curly Ralston? Is there a good reason for their violation? Learn how Chip comes to better understand the value of friendship.

____   ____   14. *Tournament Crisis:* Chip Hilton and Jimmy Chung wage a fierce contest for a starting assignment on State University's varsity basketball team. Then adversity strikes, forcing Jimmy to leave State. Can Chip use his knowledge of Chinese culture and filial piety to help the Chung family, Jimmy, and the team?

____   ____   15. *Hardcourt Upset:* Mystery and hot basketball action team up to make *Hardcourt Upset* a must-read! Can Chip help solve the rash of convenience store burglaries that threatens the reputation of one of the Hilton A. C.? Play along with Chip and his teammates as they demonstrate valor on and off the court and help their Tech rivals earn an NCAA bid.

About the Author

CLAIR BEE, who coached football, baseball, and basketball at the collegiate level, is considered one of the greatest basketball coaches of all time—both collegiate and professional. His winning percentage, 82.6, ranks first overall among any major college coaches, past or present. His name lives on forever in numerous halls of fame. The Coach Clair Bee and Chip Hilton awards are presented annually at the Basketball Hall of Fame honoring NCAA Division I college coaches and players for their commitment to education, personal character, and service to others on and off the court. Bee is the author of the twenty-three volume, best-selling Chip Hilton sports series, which has influenced many sports and literary notables, including best-selling author John Grisham.